Torment

Standing close to her, [he had to] battle an almost overp[owering urge to] arms around her and draw her near. He was honest enough to admit it was not her inner strength he wished to mold against his chest. It was her tantalizing, womanly softness.

Janine, too, found their closeness unnerving. Her senses reeled from the ease with which he had lifted her, and as she watched his face, she found it quite difficult to breathe.

Though she had spent the last three years with little or no contact with members of the opposite sex, she was woman enough to know *that* look in a man's eyes. He wanted to kiss her. And if the intense pounding beneath her ribs was anything to judge by, she was not averse to the idea.

As a matter of fact, she was having a difficult time schooling her traitorous body, for it wanted desperately to sway toward Vincent, to feel the strength of his arms and the hardness of his chest. . . .

The Righteous Rogue

Martha Kirkland

A SIGNET BOOK

SIGNET
Published by the Penguin Group
Penguin Putnam Inc., 375 Hudson Street,
New York, New York 10014, U.S.A.
Penguin Books Ltd, 27 Wrights Lane,
London W8 5TZ, England
Penguin Books Australia Ltd,
Ringwood, Victoria, Australia
Penguin Books Canada Ltd, 10 Alcorn Avenue,
Toronto, Ontario, Canada M4V 3B2
Penguin Books (N.Z.) Ltd, 182-190 Wairau Road,
Auckland 10, New Zealand

Penguin Books Ltd, Registered Offices:
Harmondsworth, Middlesex, England

First published by Signet, an imprint of Dutton Signet,
a member of Penguin Putnam Inc.

First Printing, December, 1997
10 9 8 7 6 5 4 3 2 1

Ⓢ REGISTERED TRADEMARK—MARCA REGISTRADA

Printed in the United States of America

*To all the teachers who encouraged me to ask
questions, then sent me in search of the answers.
Especially to Martha Sims Payne, who asked, Why?
Why not? and Why not you?*

Chapter 1

"What in Hades?"

Vincent Charles Thornton, the seventh Baron Thornton, stopped just inside the handsome ground-floor library of his Brook Street town house, displeasure writ plainly upon his deeply tanned face. His vexation was occasioned by the sight of a sheet of sketch paper propped against the ormolu clock on the pale marble mantelpiece—a paper that bore a pen and ink likeness of himself.

He thought he had thrown the drawing into the fire last night, after returning from a rather tedious evening spent in the company of the beautiful, though empty-headed, barque of frailty presently enjoying his protection. Fancying herself an artist, the woman had presented him with the sketch as a token of her gratitude for his having purchased a rather showy necklace of diamonds and sapphires she had declared herself unable to live without.

Owing to the subdued candlelight in the appreciative lady's bedchamber, Vincent had been unable to see much of the drawing at that time, detecting only a thin, angular visage and a head of thick, dark hair. However, once he returned to Brook Street where there was no need for subtle lighting, he came face to face with what was a disturbingly accurate rendering of himself—disturbing because the likeness could have served as well for the sixth Baron Thornton, his late father.

Seeing his father's image on the resurrected paper, Vincent's entire being filled with intense loathing. There, before him, was the same familiar jet-black hair, the same uncompromising features, the same arrogant set of the chin.

"Damnation," he muttered.

With long, angry strides, he crossed the mellowed maroon and blue of the Axminster carpet, then snatched the paper from the mantel and ripped it into a dozen pieces. After throwing the pieces into the fire, he did not move from the hearth until he saw the yellow and orange flames devour every fragment, turning them to ashes.

It had been sixteen years since he had last seen his father, and until he beheld that cursed drawing, Vincent had not realized how like his parent he had grown. How very like *Satan* he appeared.

The previous Lord Thornton had been known as Satan, a sobriquet he had earned many times over with his debauched cronies in Town, as well as with his neighbors at home in Kent. The reason for the name was obvious, for it spoke of his preference for those amusements tolerated only by the darker element of society. However, despite his reputation, and a manner that often bordered on the cruel, he was never openly rejected by the polite world, a circumstance that owed all to his vast wealth.

Vincent had been a boy of fifteen the last time he looked into that devil's cold, amber eyes. His father had just put him into the keeping of a sea captain who had been paid to see that the lad reached the island of Barbados, in the West Indies. Rage had filled the young, motherless boy at being forced to leave his home, exiled for having had the effrontery to defy his father, and as the ship slipped from its berth and headed toward the open sea, the young Vincent had prayed never again to see those amber eyes.

In that, at least, his prayers had been answered, for his father now lay buried in the peaceful graveyard behind the church at Dorking, and the eyes Vincent beheld each morning in his looking glass were gray as the waters of the Atlantic Ocean. But there was no denying his father's stamp upon the remainder of Vincent's looks. No wonder so many strangers had turned to stare at him on the streets these last two months since his return to England.

One inebriated fellow had even accosted him several nights ago, catching hold of his coatsleeve and babbling on about *the plan*, and how well it was working.

"I believe you have made a mistake," Vincent had said.

The fellow looked around him, as if afraid he might have been overheard. "Yes, yes," he said, his words slurred with drink, "you are exactly right. Must keep up the pose."

Disengaging his sleeve from the man's grasp, Vincent tried once again to get through to that wine-befogged brain. "I tell you, sir, that you are in error. Now step aside, if you please."

"That is very well done!" he said, with a wink. "Exactly the right tone. Now, if you will but continue to do as you have been, we shall soon find ourselves as rich as Croesus."

Unable to convince the gentleman with the thinning hair and the thickening middle that they were not acquainted, Vincent had been obliged to threaten to plant him a facer if he did not step out of his way.

Taken aback by the threat, the objectionable fellow had looked him over slowly; then, with dawning understanding of his mistake, had finally begged his pardon and taken himself off, all but running down the street in his haste to be gone.

"Your pardon, sir," said a voice from the far corner of the library, interrupting Vincent's unpleasant recollections. "It was I who put the drawing on the mantel."

"Devil take it!"

Startled, Vincent turned quickly, his right hand reaching inside his coat, his fingers finding the ivory hilt of the dagger he wore always upon his person.

To his surprise, the visitor was a slender youth of perhaps seventeen summers, on the verge of manhood, though his exceedingly handsome countenance had not yet lost its boyish smoothness. Almost angelic looking, the lad stood beside the French windows that opened onto the small back garden, and the morning sunlight streaming through the panes cast an otherworldly aura upon his blond hair, putting Vincent in mind of a painting by Michelangelo.

As if the visitor read his host's thoughts, he clenched his fists, while his blue eyes flashed a decidedly pugnacious dare to anyone unwise enough to comment upon his looks.

Though Vincent judged the pugnacity to be a more reliable measure of the bantling's true character than that angelic aura, still he relaxed his hold upon the dagger, moving his hand nonchalantly to straighten the lapel of his corbeau green coat, as if that had been his intention all along.

"I found the sketch on the floor, sir. I did not mean to . . ." He cleared his throat, then fell silent.

"Of course you did not," Vincent replied, as if the apology had been completed. "Let us speak no more upon the subject. Furthermore, it is I who should beg your pardon, for no one told me I had a visitor. I hope I have not kept you waiting long."

"Oh, no, sir."

"Good. The butler has been with the family for many years, and he tends to forget such things as announcing guests."

The young gentleman relaxed. "I thought that might be what had happened, for the fellow looked old as Methuselah. We have just such a one at home. The gardener. And his attic's to let, if you ask me, for he threatened to set the dogs on me a year or so back, when I chanced to pick a posy. Remembers my grandfather quite clearly, but he keeps forgetting who I am."

Deciding to stem the story before it grew too long, Vincent raised straight, black eyebrows in question. "Unlike the gardener, I do not recall you or your grandfather. Who are you?"

The lad was not at all disconcerted by so blunt a question, merely smiling in a manner that put Michelangelo's angels to shame. "I am your cousin, sir. I am Gareth Henley."

"Of course you are," Vincent said, crossing the room, his hand extended in welcome. "How unperceptive of me not to have recognized you immediately, for you have the same blue eyes as your mother. I am pleased to make your acquaintance."

Breathing a sigh of relief at his reception, Gareth watched a smile of genuine pleasure soften the harsh features of his mysterious cousin's face, warming the gray eyes that had appeared almost icy only moments ago.

"I suppose my Aunt Letitia told you I visited her in Hereford last month?"

"Yes, sir. Mother wrote me that you had come to her almost as soon as your ship landed."

After extricating himself from his cousin's strong, callused hand, Gareth accepted the invitation to be seated, sinking into the lush comfort of a brown leather chair. As for his tall cousin, he did not take the companion chair, but chose instead to sit upon the edge of a carved mahogany writing desk, his long legs stretched out in front of him, one booted foot crossed over the other.

"And now, Gareth, perhaps you should tell me how I may be of service to you."

"Service? To me, sir? I assure you I need—"

"Cut line, my boy. Your mother informed me that you were at Cambridge, and unless the scholastic life has changed considerably since I was at Eton, one does not come up to Town in the middle of the term."

"But the term is *almost* over."

"I suppose you mean almost over for everyone but you. May one hazard a guess that you have been sent down?"

"In a manner of speaking."

"Anything serious?"

"No, sir. There was a trifling matter of a sheep being hid in the bagwig's chambers, but I assure you, in this instance I was blameless."

"In *this* instance?"

"Yes, sir. I freely admitted to having taken part in the shortening of the don's bed linen just before the Easter holidays, but in the matter of the livestock, I was innocent. Actually, it was Sternhagen and Crawley who thought of the sheep, but I could hardly give them up to the bagwig. So you see—"

"Please," his cousin said, raising his hand as if to ward off confidences. "Save your explanations for your father. Tell me only how I fit into your present plans."

Gareth felt his face grow warm. How could he admit to his cousin that he had come to London for no other reason than to meet him—to see for himself this larger-than-life relative, this man who, when only a boy, had been mysteriously exiled to the other side of the world.

For years Gareth had dreamed of this moment, of becoming acquainted with the man who had traveled the Amazon River, ventured into places without names, braved the dangers of hostile tribesmen, and endured the perils of wild beasts. The instant he had received his mother's letter relating the visit, Gareth had known he must come, must look upon the face of the man who had figured in all his boyhood dreams of adventure.

But how could he say all this to the man himself?

"Sir, I—" A knock at the library door granted him his reprieve.

"Enter," his cousin called.

There was a great deal of fumbling at the doorknob before the portal was opened by the ancient butler who had admitted Gareth to the house. "Begging your lordship's pardon," he said, glancing down at the silver salver he held in his hand, "but a gentleman wishes to speak with you."

Not waiting for the elderly servant to make his way across the room, Vincent met him, lifting the white visiting card from the small tray. "Neville," he said, reading the name upon the pasteboard. "I do not believe I know anyone by that name. Did the gentleman state his business?"

Before the butler could answer, the door was pushed wide, revealing a silver-haired gentleman in a well-cut gray coat and dark pantaloons. In his hand he carried his hat, his walking stick, and a pair of gray kid gloves. Raising these items on high, he fairly shouted at Vincent. "Try to pretend you do not recognize the name, you blackguard. It will not serve, I tell you, for you know full well who I am, and why I have come."

Wrinkling his nose as if smelling something unpleasant, he continued, "I might have known how it would be once I heard of your return to England. You . . . you Spawn of Satan!"

Gareth stared open-mouthed as the gentleman railed at Vincent. Only with the final insult did his cousin react, though his sole show of emotion was a slight drawing together of those jet black eyebrows.

"Sir," Vincent said, his voice quiet, yet icy cold. "Exchanging insults will get us nowhere. Kindly state your business, for I assure you I have no idea why you have come."

The visitor spoke through tightly clenched teeth. "Charles Neville is my grandson. Do you dare to tell me you do not recognize his name?"

"You may believe me when I tell you that I have not had the pleasure."

"Not had the pleasure!" The man swore. "You must think me in my dotage, else you would not attempt to gull me with such tales, you villainous cur."

Though Vincent's voice was very soft, the muscle that twitched in his jaw belied his outward calm. "Have a care what you call me. Though I do not consider you to be in your dotage, it is only your age that allows you to say these things to me with impunity. Even so, my patience is not without limits."

"I say no more than the truth, for you are a villain. It was not enough that you lured my grandson into a gaming hell and cheated him of his money. No! When Charles accused you of fuzzing the cards, you took your revenge by lying in wait for him in the alley outside the hell, where you beat him within an inch of his life."

The anger seemed to go out of the older man, and his lips trembled. "He might be lying there yet if it were not for the kindness of the unidentified gentleman who put him into a hackney, paying the jarvey from his own pocket. Even so, Charles arrived home half dead. His grandmother is at his bedside now, praying for him to regain consciousness."

"And when did this beating take place?" Vincent asked.

"You know full well when it occurred. It was late last evening."

Vincent stepped quite close to the man, and for a moment Gareth thought he meant to place his hand upon the gentleman's shoulder. He did not do so; though when he spoke, his tone was gentle, compassionate. "You have my sympathies for your grandson's misfortune, sir, but I assure you I have never met him. Not last evening. Not ever. And should you require proof of my whereabouts, it can be furnished. For yesterday afternoon and most of the evening, I was in the company of a friend."

"Yes," Neville said, his anger rising again, "you were with that worthless fribble, Sir Burton Morgan. Everyone knows that you and he are as thick as thieves, and I have it on good authority that the two of you were seen together early yesterday evening."

"Sir Burton Morgan?" Vincent shook his head. "Your informant is mistaken, for I am acquainted with no such person."

"Liar!"

Before Gareth knew what was happening, Mr. Neville lifted his gloves and dealt Vincent a sharp slap across the face. "I shall have satisfaction for this," he said. "My friends shall call upon yours."

Chapter 2

Bexham, East Sussex, May 5, 1815

"In my next life," Miss Janine Morgan muttered angrily as she scanned the empty yard of the Red Hart Inn, "I shall have the good sense to be born independently wealthy."

Not that she embraced the theory of multiple lives, of course. She had never even heard the phrase until a few months ago, when on the occasion of her twenty-fourth birthday Cousin Hortense had presented her with a book on Eastern philosophies. Her elderly cousin, Church of England to the very marrow of her bones, had purchased the volume not because she wished to investigate other idealogies, but because the moth-eaten little book was the cheapest thing she could find among the various items dumped upon a table in the rear of the booksellers off Market Place, in Bath.

A woman of parsimonious inclination where her unpaid companion was concerned, Miss Hortense Morgan had presented the gift; then, after complaining endlessly about the expenditure of an entire shilling, had insisted that Janine read aloud to her every last page of the book.

"You being met, miss?" the freckle-faced young ostler asked as he lifted down her corded trunk from the boot of the stagecoach, depositing both the trunk and a battered valise on the hard-packed ground quite near her feet.

"It would appear not."

Janine looked around her once again at the inn yard. It was deserted except for the ostler, the coachman, the burly fellow who was busily harnessing a fresh team to the stagecoach, and a nondescript yellow dog who lay half asleep near the coach house doors, too lazy to do more than roll his eyes at what was a common activity at the Red Hart Inn. Though Janine had written her brother that she would be arriving from Bath on May fifth, he had sent no one to the inn to meet her.

"Would you be wanting to hire a gig, then?" the lad persisted. "The smithy be just down the street, and I'd be happy to run over there and see to the hiring. See you was given a fair price too."

He would never know how fervently she wished she could afford such luxuries as hired conveyances. Unfortunately, her reticule contained a one pound note, a sixpence, and two farthings, which was the sum total of her wealth.

It had come as a severe blow to Janine when, four weeks ago, Cousin Hortense had gone to her heavenly reward, obviously taking with her whatever treasures she had stored up here on earth. Though the old harridan had promised Janine future recompense in lieu of a monthly salary, not even a token bequest had been mentioned in the will. Left with nothing but the clothes she had brought with her when she quit Bexham three years earlier, Janine had been obliged to write to her brother for assistance, explaining her difficulties and begging him to send her sufficient money for a stagecoach ticket home.

To her dismay, Sir Burton Morgan had not replied to any of his sister's letters. Nor, so it would seem, had he taken note of her final missive, informing him that she had been obliged to sell their mother's cameo brooch to purchase the needed ticket, and that she would be arriving in Bexham the following Tuesday. Brother and sister had never been close, but Burton's blatant indifference to her welfare was a painful revelation to Janine.

Yes. I definitely intend to be rich in my next life!

"The gig, miss?"

Calling herself to attention, she gazed at the tall, leggy youth whose bright red hair and copious sprinkling of copper freckles branded him as one of the dozen or so McFee offspring. Which one, she could not even guess; not one of the older children, obviously, for he did not seem to recognize her.

"Thank you," she said, "but I do not need a gig. I shall walk."

Young McFee looked up into the afternoon sky. "Rain'll be here soon, miss."

Unable to stop herself, Janine followed his lead, searching for the sun that had played hide and seek the entire day. As far as she could see, the sky looked no more threatening now than it had earlier. "What makes you think it will rain?"

"Seen a flock of rooks this morning, diving to the ground. Up real high, they were, and as they dove, the sound was like a gust of wind." Looking at her as if that explained it all, he added, "That always 'tokens rain."

Praying this interesting bit of country lore was fallible, Janine bid him take her trunk inside. "Tell the innkeeper that someone from Morgan House will pick it up tomorrow."

As if surprised by her words, the youth's mouth dropped open. "*Morgan House*, did you say?"

"I did, for that is my destination."

"But there b'aint—"

"Stop your dawdling," yelled the burly fellow who had just finished harnessing the fresh team. "There be 'orses waiting in the stable, and if I know ought of cattle, they b'aint rubbing themselves down. Nor fetching their own water, I'm thinking."

Smiling apologetically at her, young McFee pulled his forelock politely, lifted the trunk to his shoulder, then hurried with it toward the inn, leaving Janine standing beside the coach, wondering what the lad had been about to say about Morgan House. Lost in thought, she was surprised when the driver snapped his whip above the heads of the fresh horses, and the stagecoach lurched forward, obliging her to jump back out of harm's way.

"Dash it all!" she remarked inelegantly.

The horses picked up speed quickly as they neared the bottom of the high street, and in little more than a minute, all that was left of the coach that had brought her home to East Sussex was the dust that swirled in its wake. Janine stood alone in the inn yard—alone save for the yellow dog who had finally roused from his *ennui* and was now barking excitedly at the empty road.

All too aware that there was nothing to be gained by standing about, Janine tightened the strings of her yellow straw Dutch bonnet and fastened the frogs of her brown poplin pelisse, pulling the material close against her chest to protect herself from the wind that was freshening.

When Janine lifted the valise, she found it heavier than she remembered, and for an instant she considered leaving it with her trunk. Unfortunately, she dared not, for she knew she would need the night-clothes and toilet articles once she reached home.

After three years' absence, it was quite possible that nothing she had left behind would be usable.

"Morgan House is but a distance of three miles," she chided herself. "Have you grown so accustomed to town life that you cannot manage a brisk walk in the country with one small case in tow?"

Hoping the answer to that question was *no*, she passed beneath the sign upon which was painted a leaping red hart and began walking north, following the high street past McFee's saddlery and Jem Aylsworth's blacksmith shop—neither of which had altered appreciably during her absence.

Reaching the end of the village, she spied the first change, an establishment that was not as she remembered it. Standing off by itself was a two-story stone building, once an inn and alehouse. In years past it had been a busy, noisy place, frequented by sometimes unsavory clientele, but now it stood silent, untenanted. The front door was boarded up, the roof was in dire need of fresh thatching, and the windows were so grime-encrusted there was no way anyone could have seen in or out of them.

There were no signs of life—no voices raised in drunken laughter, no gray smoke curling from the chimneys—and yet Janine had the eerie feeling that she was being watched. Not wanting to prolong the sensation, she sped up her pace, leaving the alehouse behind and hurrying toward the centuries-old stone bridge that crossed a deep and rather swiftly moving brook.

Once she had traversed the bridge, Janine found the view much more to her liking, for on both sides of the road the hedgerows were thick with stinging nettle, and on the rolling hills beyond, cow parsley waved in the wind, the dark green of its fernlike leaves appearing almost black against the delicate white flowers.

As she passed a magnificent spreading oak tree, a startled rook shouted its harsh *caw* before taking flight, the midnight black of its graceful wings soon becoming indistinguishable in the ever-darkening sky. The sun had completely disappeared, and in its place a distant cloud, dark and ominous, seemed to be moving in Janine's direction, as if mocking her for her disrespect of the young ostler's prediction of rain.

If the sun had chosen to shine, Janine might have enjoyed her walk, but with the clouds growing more threatening, and an unmistakable roll of thunder sounding in the distance, her primary concern was reaching Morgan House before the rain came. Knowing how quickly a downpour could turn even a decent road into a quagmire, she hurried her steps, and in little more than an hour she turned onto the deeply rutted lane that led to her home.

Long before the last half mile was accomplished, however, the first raindrop fell. Soon a second and a third drop followed the first. They were icy missiles, and they pelted Janine like liquid rocks hurled from on high.

Holding out her gloved hand, she watched the damp splashes soak into the cream cotton. "It wanted only this," she muttered, looking from the glove to the heavens. "Is the entire world being treated to dismal weather, or is this karma mine alone?"

With the last three years as her guideline, she was much inclined to believe that the fates had singled her out.

"Of course," she muttered, "one always has a choice. I could have gone south from the inn and stopped off at Dyrham Cottage. It was nothing but pride that kept me from doing so."

If she had gone to the cottage, instead of letting pride stay her feet, Miss Evangeline Craven might at this moment be pouring her a cup of strong tea; she might even have suggested driving Janine to Morgan House in her pony trap. Conjecture only. The likelihood of either of those two things happening depended upon whether or not Miss Craven was still on speaking terms with her former student. With no money for posting letters, Janine's correspondence with her friend and former schoolmistress had ceased shortly after her sojourn to Bath.

Lost in her thoughts of Dyrham Cottage and the cup of tea, Janine was unprepared for the earth-shattering clap of thunder that exploded overhead, shaking her from the soles of her jean half boots all the way to the thick brown hair secured neatly at the nape of her neck. Unable to stop herself, she cried out. Before she could still her trembling lips, the first explosion was followed by another, the second even louder than the first.

The random raindrops became more plentiful with each succeeding moment, spattering the brown poplin of her pelisse. Before Janine knew what was happening, the steadily increasing volume turned into a veritable wall of water, a liquid barricade that slowed her progress and reduced vision to mere inches.

Cold, punishing rain beat against her face. Relentlessly the water gushed down her neck, continuing its flow inside the collar of her pelisse and her dress, and trickling between her breasts, stopping only when it became lost somewhere inside her shift. In a very short time, the several layers of her clothing were soaked through, chilling her all the way to the bone.

Not content with drenching her, the downpour turned the rutted lane to slick, flowing ooze. Walking was impossible. Conversely, slipping and falling were maddeningly easy, and before Janine reached the low stone wall that announced her arrival at her destination, she had lost her footing three times, landing on all fours in the mire. Her face, her gloves, and the entire front of her pelisse were soon covered in mud.

At the wrought-iron gates that gave access to the long, straight carriageway, she breathed a sigh of relief. Too happy to be home to notice that the left gate hung drunkenly, its lynch pin obviously lost for some time, she grasped the right, using it to assist her to remain upright until she could step upon the gravel of the carriageway.

Though the gravel was sparse, and in bad need of regrading, it was not until Janine had almost reached the front entrance that she became aware of how desolate the estate appeared. Even through the rain that came down in sheets, obscuring her vision, she could see the neglect.

Never a beautiful edifice, the pink brick house had owed what charm it possessed to the symmetry of its two-level central structure and the two single-story wings that extended to the rear. Unfortunately, symmetry was no match for the depressing sight of sagging shutters and an upper floor window stuffed with rags to keep out the weather. As well, a number of bricks from the right front chimney had fallen to the ground, and that corner of the roof appeared to have lost some tiles.

Stepping beneath the trellis arch that framed the front door, Janine noticed that the vines were choked with old wood. Obviously, no one had bothered to prune them for several seasons. But why? And why had Burton not seen to the repair of the chimney and the roof?

The house had been in want of repairs for some time, and just before she left for Bath, she had begged her brother to have at least the most pressing needs seen to. Apparently, he had ignored her requests.

"Burton," she muttered through clenched teeth, "what were you thinking of to let the place fall into such disrepair? Surely you know that this house is all we have left of our heritage, and of our parents."

But what was the good of talking to herself. Even if Burton were here, he would pay her no heed, for her brother embraced a lifestyle quite beyond the rather modest income derived from the estate. A gambler, he was constantly on the verge of financial ruin. But in that, he was no different from their father.

Sir George had always been under the hatches; though he had never let things get this far out of hand. Or more accurately, their mother had never allowed it. Somehow, Lady Morgan had always found a way to settle the worst of the debts owed their creditors, with enough money left over to pay the servants' wages.

"And speaking of the servants," Janine muttered, "where in heaven's name are they?"

After pounding upon the door for what seemed like hours, with no response from within, she began to wonder if they could hear her above the noise of the storm. Perhaps they were all in the kitchen having their tea before a nice fire. Janine envied them. Though as cold and miserable as she felt, tea and a fire would not suffice; nothing would warm her but a soak in a hot bath.

The image of herself languishing in a hip bath filled with hot, steaming water, encouraged her to knock one last time. However, when there was still no answer, she decided to walk around to the left wing, the wing that housed the kitchen and the servants' rooms.

To her relief, the kitchen door was unlocked, and as she lifted the latch and pushed the heavy door open,

she recalled the many times she had come in this way
when she was a child. Remembering the big, warm
room with its huge fireplace, and the wonderful
yeasty aroma of bread baking in the brick oven, she
smiled, thinking how glad she was to be home, and
how surprised Mrs. Polson and the kitchen maids
would be to see her.

It was Janine who got the surprise.

As she stepped inside the kitchen, the smile died
upon her lips. There was no welcoming cookfire
warming the large room; not even a lone candle burning upon the oak dresser to brighten the dimness. Nor
were there any delicious aromas floating upon the air.
Instead, the room was dank and still, and it smelled
suspiciously like mouse droppings.

And it was empty. No housekeeper. No maids.

Judging by the depth of the dust upon the scarred
deal table, and the density of the cobwebs hanging
from the ceiling, Janine doubted that anyone had been
there in months. Perhaps years.

No wonder the young ostler had looked so stunned
when she mentioned sending someone from Morgan
House for her trunk. If the lad had not been inter-
rutped, he might have told her that the house was deserted. No; not deserted—it had been abandoned.
And if the remainder of the place was in the same deplorable state as the servants' wing, it would need a
fortune to make it habitable again.

Something—perhaps it was the knowledge that she
had no place else to go, and no money to travel to
some other destination even if such a place existed—
gave her hope that the remainder of the house would
look better. With that unfounded optimism spurring
her to action, Janine set her valise, her reticule, and
her sodden bonnet upon the filthy table and hurried
toward the main part of the house.

Upon reaching the vestibule, she paused for a moment at the bottom of the once-handsome staircase. Even in the fading light, she could not fail to notice the evidence of damp upon walls that had been stripped of every last painting.

Looking in vain for the Holbein that had been part of her mother's dowry, Janine voiced a most unladylike oath.

"So that is how my brother has been supporting himself. He has been stripping the house of everything of value."

Hoping she had seen the worst, she climbed the stairs and walked to her old bedchamber, a room she remembered as being small but charmingly decorated, with delicate yellow bed hangings and a lovely view of the back garden.

Here, too, she was destined for disappointment, and as she stood in the doorway looking at what had once been a young girl's private domain, unshed tears stung her eyes.

She did not enter the room, but it was not the half dozen puddles upon the floor that stayed her feet, nor even the filthy hangings. What held her rooted to the spot was the mice that squeaked at her intrusion into their territory, a few scurrying to the far corners of the room, but most disappearing inside the stuffing of the disintegrating mattress. With a shudder, Janine shut the door and sped back down to the kitchen.

Not even bothering to dust off the ancient basket-weave chair, she collapsed at the table, leaning her head against her valise. Too stunned by the enormity of what she had found, she did not cry, but merely closed her eyes, wondering what she was to do now.

It was too late to return to the village today, for it would be dark within the hour, but at first light tomorrow she would go to Dyrham Cottage, to Miss

Evangeline Craven. She would ask her old friend for shelter for a few days, just until she could find employment of some kind. But that was tomorrow, and before Janine could seek the comfort of Dyrham Cottage, this evening and night had to be got through.

Both hungry and thirsty, she finally rose from the table and searched the larder for something—anything—to eat. She found nothing.

Thinking the stillroom off the housekeeper's bedchamber might yield a bottle of Mrs. Polson's dandelion wine, Janine went there next. Again she was disappointed, for there was no wine. However, her exploration was not without profit. Upon one of the shelves she found a battered pewter candlestick that still held the stub of a work candle, and a phosphorus box containing two sulphur-tipped matches, both still dry.

Cheered by the knowledge that she would not be obliged to pass the entire night in the dark, she decided to look into the housekeeper's room to see if it had fared any better than her own chamber. Opening the door just far enough to peep inside, she was delighted to discover that the simply furnished bedroom appeared in tolerably good condition.

To get a better look, she pushed the door wider, though she chose to remain just on the other side of the threshold. The first thing she noticed was that the plain walnut tent bed appeared neat, almost as if the faded counterpane had been straightened that very day. As well, the musty smell that permeated the rest of the house was much less noticeable in this room.

With the memory still fresh in her mind of the inhabited mattress abovestairs, Janine stamped her feet several times. Happily, no small creatures scurried about in reaction to the noise, so she decided she would approach the bed slowly, give it a sharp kick with the sole of her boot, then jump back if necessary. Should the bed prove empty, she meant to light the candle and search the dim corners of the room for vermin. If none were present, she had every intention of removing her wet clothes, crawling beneath the warm covers, and remaining there until morning.

When she entered the room, her thoughts were centered upon the task before her, and her need to complete it while a hint of daylight still showed at the window. Even so, before she had taken a half dozen steps, some inner voice told her she had made a mistake in assuming that only four-legged creatures might be hiding in the darkness.

Realizing that someone stood behind the door, she turned to run, but as she did so, a hand reached out and clamped over her mouth, the fingers digging into her flesh. At the same time, a strong arm grasped her around the waist, lifting her completely off the floor and yanking her against a rock-hard chest. More frightened than she had ever been in her life, Janine began to struggle, clawing at the hand upon her face and kicking, albeit wildly, in hopes of dealing her captor a blow to the shins.

"Be still," the man ordered, his mouth so close to her ear that she could feel his warm breath upon her cheek.

When she continued to struggle, he tightened the arm around her waist, forcing the breath from her lungs and making her fear she would soon lose consciousness. "Be still," he said again. "I have no wish to harm you."

With her pulse beating like a drum inside her head, and her lungs burning for want of oxygen, she went limp against him. Immediately he loosened his hold enough to allow her to gulp deep breaths of air.

"If you give me your promise not to scream," he said, "I will release you."

Janine nodded her head in agreement. It was the logical thing to do, for with no one to hear her but her captor, screaming would have been an exercise in futility.

Cautiously he eased his hand from her mouth, ready to put it back if she made a noise. When he saw she meant to keep her promise, he let his hand fall to his side. "Are you alone?" he asked.

Too frightened to speak, she nodded once again.

Obviously satisfied that she told the truth, the man slowly relaxed his grip upon her waist, allowing her to regain her footing before he set her free.

"Go sit down," he said, giving her a nudge toward the bed.

With legs as wobbly as India rubber, Janine crossed the bare floor, then sat on the edge of the bed, holding to the footboard with both hands as though clinging to a life line. While she watched, the man bent and retrieved the pewter candlestick and the phosphorus box she had dropped, then strode over to the bombé bureau, his footsteps oddly quiet for such a tall man. When he turned his back to her to light the candle, she took the opportunity to study him, from his leather top boots all the way to the thick, jet-black hair that touched the collar of his shirt.

He wore no coat, and with only the thin white lawn of his shirt covering his broad shoulders and long tapered back, it was easy to see that he was strong and fit. He must weigh at least twelve stone, and from the looks of his well-toned arms and legs, he had no need of the knife she had seen him slip surreptitiously into the leather sheath across his chest.

Vincent felt her watching him. In the jungle, where the hunter can easily become the prey, a wise man learned how to feel eyes upon him, or he did not survive. Not that the half-drowned woman before him posed any threat to his survival; she was too frightened to do more than stare. Beneath the mud that all but obscured her face, she looked pale enough to faint, and he felt a pang of regret at having given her what was probably the scare of her life.

If the truth be known, she had given him a few bad moments as well. The din of the rain must have covered the sound of her arrival, for he had not even known she was in the house until he heard her enter the stillroom. Another minute and she would have caught him stretched out upon the bed.

Deuce take it! Now what am I to do?

He could hear her breathing. It was ragged, as though she had run a long way, and not wanting to frighten her further, he turned and perched on the edge of the dresser, his arms folded across his chest.

"Why are you here?" he asked. "Did no one ever tell you the trouble a female can get into by traveling alone?"

She did not answer, but continued to regard him, the fear of a moment ago slowly giving way to puzzlement. With her brow knit in question, she studied his chin, his mouth, his nose, examining each feature with care until the puzzled expression finally vanished.

To Vincent's surprise, her brown eyes suddenly flashed with anger. Her chin lifted obstinately and her backbone straightened. Without uttering a word, she rose from the bed and stepped very close to him, never lowering her gaze from his. Before he guessed what she had in mind, she drew back her hand and slapped him across the face as hard as she could.

"What the—"

"If you ever frighten me like that again, Zachary Flynn, I promise you, I will do the world a favor and put a bullet through your worthless hide."

Chapter 3

Vincent Thornton rubbed his cheek with the back of his hand, the week's worth of stubble making a scraping sound in the stillness that followed the woman's threat. Had the world gone mad? Everyone he met lately seemed bent on slapping his face.

No. Not *his* face.

The woman, at least, had thought she was striking someone named Zachary Flynn. She seemed quite certain of the fact.

"Where is Burton?" she asked,

Burton! There was a name Vincent recognized. It was on the chance that he might encounter Sir Burton Morgan that Vincent was moldering away in this rat's nest of a house. The property belonged to Morgan, and the man was his only lead to the person who had very nearly murdered the Neville lad, a crime for which Vincent was being blamed.

"What makes you think I know where Burton may be found?"

The look she gave him was filled with contempt. "Parry a question with a question. I see your years in his Majesty's army were not wasted, for you have acquired the art of evasiveness."

Ah. Here was information that might prove useful. The woman was obviously well acquainted with this man called Flynn. If Vincent could keep her talking, perhaps she would furnish him with a clue to the fellow's whereabouts.

"And you," he said, the words spoken softly, his purpose to charm her if he could, "have acquired something even more interesting. You have grown quite beautiful."

To his surprise, she blushed. Even beneath the mud, he could see the heat rush to her face.

"I will thank you to keep your compliments to yourself, Zach Flynn, for I want no part of them. I am not one of those foolish village girls who pine for your attention."

Vincent put his hand over his heart. "A man can but hope, fair lady."

"Balderdash! Do not make a cake of yourself on my account. 'Tis wasted effort, I assure you. I did not like you five years ago, when I saw you last, and absence has not imbued my heart with any greater degree of fondness. You were a rogue and a cheat then, and I cherish no great hopes that being a soldier of the line has improved either your morals or your desire to pursue an honest career."

Vincent had watched with some enjoyment while Miss Mud-on-the-Face delivered her scathing reading of Zach Flynn's character, and despite his partiality toward soft-spoken females with blond hair and blue eyes, he had to admit there was something arresting in the spirit of this dark-haired miss. It might have been the fire that burned in her large brown eyes, or, as illogical as it seemed, it might well have been the way she looked him over from head to toe, contempt uppermost in her assessment. If Zach Flynn was everything she believed him to be, Vincent admired her for not liking the rascal.

When she continued to stare at him, however, he decided to give her a taste of her own medicine.

Slowly he looked her over, working his way down from her face to her mud-caked half-boots, then back up again, pausing when he encountered those parts of her figure that most pleased him. Because she possessed gently rounded hips, with a waist that nipped in quite fetchingly, and a bosom any man would find appealing, he paused often, enjoying his perusal.

When he looked into her face once again, she had grown quite pink, and if the angry set of her mouth was any indication, she was contemplating slapping him a second time.

"Allow me to inform you, sir, that I do not find your attention pleasing. My brother may choose to associate with you, though why Burton should do so I have never understood, but I retain a few of our parents' standards."

So. Sir Burton was her brother. That explained at least part of the riddle of why she was in this place alone.

She had continued to speak, and though Vincent missed part of what she said, he had no difficulty in guessing the gist of her comments—she was not pleased to find him in her house. "So if your mother's cottage still stands, I should be obliged if you would take yourself there and leave me in peace."

"You would send me out on such a night as this? Madam, I must protest. Such cruel words sit ill upon such soft lips."

Janine had to look away from his handsome countenance, for she found to her dismay that she was no more immune to the rogue's honeyed words than any other of the females who resided in Bexham. Hoping to keep him from realizing how susceptible she was to his flirtation, she turned her attention to the sheathed knife quite near his fingertips.

"You may call me cruel if you wish, sir, but I do not believe you will come to any great harm if you leave my home." She gazed pointedly at the knife. "Though I can easily credit that your enemies are legion, a man in possession of such a menacing-looking weapon should be capable of defending himself."

"Against my enemies, yes." He patted the sheath. "Unfortunately, this little bit of steel offers no protection against the elements."

"Nonetheless, I must insist you go."

"Have you no heart?" he asked softly. "No ounce of that tender kindness that resides within the feminine breast?"

Janine felt herself flush from head to toe. And to add insult to injury, the scoundrel smiled, leaving her in no doubt that he was all too aware of her warmth.

"You cannot stay," she said, though even to her own ears, the pronouncement lacked conviction. "It . . . it would be unseemly."

An unholy light shone from his gray eyes—eyes that appeared even more startling against his deeply tanned skin. "Unseemly? You mean because I am a man, and you are a woman . . . alone?"

Somehow, the tone of his voice was almost seductive, the inference of the last word that their isolation might prove mutually enjoyable. While she marshaled her thoughts in preparation to deliver a scathing setdown, he angered her further by chuckling.

"Before you toss me out in such a cavalier manner, madam, allow me to inform you that I have gifts with which to seduce even the most reluctant hostess."

Seduce! "Why you . . . you . . ."

His smile crinkled the skin at the outer corners of his eyes, a circumstance that made him appear almost boyishly innocent, and at the same time devilishly dangerous.

"I have tea," he whispered. "And thick, crusty

bread. Of course, the cheese is slightly strong for the educated palate, but I think you will not find it totally contemptible."

At the mention of food, Janine experienced a most unpleasant gnawing sensation in the pit of her stomach.

She had not eaten since last evening, at the coaching inn, and even then she had not been given enough time to finish the meal. Almost as soon as the food was served, the driver had yelled his intention of leaving within two minutes. At the coachman's announcement, the innkeeper had rushed forward and begun removing the plates from the table, reminding the passengers that no one was allowed to take food beyond the door. Even though several of the travelers had muttered angrily of collusion to cheat them of their pre-paid meals, the plates were whisked away nonetheless. Janine had managed to gulp only a few bites before her meal was plucked from before her.

"Did you say, bread?" she asked.

When he nodded, Janine warned herself to beware, not to walk into the devil's trap. "And cheese?"

"And tea. Nothing fancy, mind you. Just a simple bohea purchased in London a few days ago from the Berry Brothers on St. James's Street. Of course, you may be a connoisseur, and find bohea much too commonplace for your taste. But I like it. To me, it is as fine a beverage as may be found anyplace. And the aroma!" He kissed his fingers dramatically. "You will agree, I am certain, that while it is steeping, black tea emits a full-bodied fragrance that is particularly—"

"Sir!" Janine said, her throat suddenly so dry she had difficulty swallowing, "you do not play fair."

With the hint of a smile, he said, "Where women are concerned, a man dare not play fair. After all, you ladies hold all the cards."

"Stuff!" she uttered inelegantly. " 'Tis a man's world, sir, and well you know it!"

"That depends upon the man." He paused. "And the woman."

Once again he forestalled her retort by continuing, "As to who is or is not playing fair, upon that score, permit me to remind you that it was not *I* who threatened to put *you* out in the storm."

With her stomach growling in protest, Janine felt less and less inclined to bandy words with him, and suspecting that she would come out the loser in the long run, she gave in with as much grace as possible. "You may stay until the rain abates. But take heed, Zach Flynn, the moment it stops, out you go."

He made her a gallant bow. "You are kindness itself, fair lady."

Janine drank half her tea, then set the chipped cup upon the table and sliced herself another slab of the dark, crusty bread, spreading it generously with cheese before taking a large, satisfying bite. "Yum," she said, as she licked an errant crumb from her lips. "Delicious."

Though he watched her tongue retrieve the crumb, making her wish she had had enough sense to keep it between her teeth, he said nothing, merely poured himself another tea and added enough to her cup to raise the liquid to the rim.

Actually, he had spoken little since Janine had agreed to share his food. Obviously aware of what needed to be done, he had gone about the business of fetching in wood and laying the fire, leaving her to search for cups and plates among the pile of cracked and chipped earthenware that had been left in the oak dresser. While he had held lighted kindling up the flue to encourage it to draw, she had wiped the dust from the table and cleaned the crockery as best she could.

Her task finished much quicker than his, she had sat in one of the scuffed Windsor chairs and watched him work at getting the blaze started, unashamedly staring at his back as he bent before the fireplace.

Through the thin white lawn of his shirt, she observed the fluid motion of his muscles as they bunched and relaxed each time he reached forward. Fascinated by a masculine beauty she had previously seen only in pictures of Greek statues, Janine had looked her fill of him, desisting only when she recalled Cousin Hortense's often repeated animadversions upon the subject of maiden ladies who made by-words of themselves by gazing like moonlings at comely gentlemen.

"Such women are pathetic at best," the bitter old harridan had said, "and at their worst, they are disgusting."

Vowing never to give her cousin ammunition with which to assail her, Janine had schooled her eyes not to stray toward any of the few personable gentlemen who came in her way. Even so, Cousin Hortense had reminded her time and again not to make a spectacle of herself.

"You are quite past your prayers, as the saying goes," Cousin Hortense had reminded her, "and even if you were possessed of a dowry—which I take leave to remind you, you are not—for a woman of your age to be encouraging attention from gentlemen goes far beyond what is pleasing. If you should do so, you would accomplish nothing save putting me to the blush and making a laughingstock of yourself."

With her cousin's words fresh in her mind, Janine turned her back on Zach Flynn, promising herself not to look at him again unless it was absolutely necessary, and to do nothing that would cause him to think her either pathetic or disgusting.

Not that I care what he thinks!

"Do you know what I think?" he asked, startling her out of her unpleasant recollections, and causing her to swallow unwisely, nearly choking on a rather large bite of bread and cheese. Unable to speak, she merely shook her head in response to his question.

Setting his cup down, he pushed his empty plate toward the center of the table. "I think it would be unwise for me to leave you here alone."

When she would have protested, he bid her listen to his reasoning. "Anyone might walk through that door. Highwaymen. Gypsies. Gaining entrance to this house is mere child's play."

"*You* obviously found it easy enough."

"Quite so," he agreed, not the least put off by her waspish tone. "And I am certain you remember the unfortunate circumstances of *our* meeting."

Janine had not forgotten. Unaccountably, merely recalling the incident made it difficult for her to take a deep breath.

She felt again the sensation of being pulled against his chest, his strong arm fast around her waist. Now, however, aware that she had nothing to fear from him, she relived not her struggle to be free, but the feel of his arm holding her close, and the heat emanating from his powerful body.

"Of course you remember," he said. "And since I cannot believe you would wish to be frightened twice in one evening, I propose that you make use of the housekeeper's room, while I remain here in the kitchen. In that way, I can keep the fire going and watch the rear entrance at the same time."

"But—"

"If you are concerned for your virtue, Miss Morgan,

please believe me, you need have no fear. Not from me, in any event."

Well! There was candor.

Janine lowered her gaze to the tea leaves in her cup, unwilling for Zach Flynn to read her emotions, more insulted than she cared to admit by his assurances as to her safety from him. He had as much as told her that he found her unappealing, not in the same category as the beauties who constantly pursued him.

As though I had the least wish to join in the chase!

"What say you?" he asked. "Shall I stay?"

The question was asked casually enough, yet Janine had the odd feeling that remaining here was of some importance to him—important in a way that had nothing to do with her.

With a shrug of her shoulders, she said, "Do what you will."

Rising with as much dignity as she could command while still clad in wet clothing, she walked over to the fireplace and removed a small piece of kindling from the wood box. Using it for a spill, she touched the kindling to the gently dancing flames until it caught fire, then cupped her free hand around it to shield the small flame from any sudden gust of wind.

Without a backward glance, or an exchange of mutual wishes for sound sleep, she quit the room.

A minute later, when she was lighting the candle stub that had been left on the bombé bureau, he tapped at the open door. Not waiting for permission to enter, he walked directly to her and set a tin washbowl and a cloth beside the candle.

"We did not use all the hot water for the tea, and I thought perhaps you might want it."

"Yes. I do. Th-thank you."

Standing so close to him in what she now thought of as her bedchamber, Janine felt suddenly shy. Foolish beyond permission, of course, for they had stood in this exact spot scarcely more than an hour ago, and at that time she had indulged in no missish displays of reticence. Yet this was different somehow. More intimate.

He must have felt it, too, for he backed away from her.

"Have you soap?" he asked.

She nodded.

"Then I will bid you peaceful dreams."

Before she could reply, Zach Flynn turned and walked away, closing the door behind him, the soft click of the latch sounding loud in the sudden silence.

Though she was to wonder at her actions later, it did not occur to Janine to hunt for a key or push any furniture against the door. It never entered her mind that her uninvited guest would behave in any but an honorable manner. Why this should be so, she could not say, for Zach Flynn was a rogue in every sense of the word.

"Give over thinking about the man!" she muttered angrily.

Hearing again Cousin Hortense's admonition not to make a laughingstock of herself, Janine lifted her valise onto the bed, unbuckled the strap, and unpacked her night rail, her brush, and her cake of soap. Loosening the tapes of her rose merino carriage dress, she removed the damp frock and hung it upon one of the wall pegs beside her muddy pelisse. Within ten minutes she was washed, clad in her warm gown, and snuggled beneath the cover, her unbound hair spread about the pillow.

Her last cognizant thought before she surrendered to sleep was of Zach Flynn, and of his unflattering assurance that her virtue was safe with him.

"In my next life," she said, her eyes blinking sleepily, "I shall have the foresight to be born devastatingly beautiful. So beautiful that I shall drive men insane."

In the kitchen, Vincent leaned back in the uncomfortable wooden chair, his booted feet propped upon the table and his thoughts upon the woman who slept in the room he had meant to occupy this evening. He could hardly begrudge her the use of her own home, of course, but he wished she had not shown up at this time. Even though she had supplied him with much needed information about the man he sought—albeit, unintentionally—he was less than pleased to find himself alone with a young woman of birth and breeding.

Especially an unmarried woman.

Tread softly, Vincent, old boy, for behind that door lies trouble. If the lady should ever discover that you possess a title, you might as well present your leg for the shackle.

He could do worse, he supposed, than be caught in parson's mousetrap with Miss Morgan, for she was a lady of intelligence and refinement, and not so set up in her own conceit that she could not dine upon bread and cheese without complaint. And if she cleaned up as well as he suspected, she would prove to be a damned fine-looking woman.

But the thing was, he did not wish to marry. Not now. Not until he had completed the task for which he had returned to England. Perhaps not ever.

Unlike most gentlemen, Vincent felt no overweening obligation to set up his nursery, for he owed nothing to his father's name. In fact, he believed the world would be a better place if "Satan" Thornton were forgotten altogether. As for the title, it would not distress Vincent in the least to see the barony pass into oblivion.

With the possible exception of his mother's sister, his Aunt Letitia, there was no one left to care whether or not he took a bride, so he could please himself upon the subject.

At the moment, all he wanted was to clear his own name; otherwise, his request to appear before the Royal Geographic Committee would be denied. He must find the man who had been impersonating him and take the scoundrel back to London to answer for his crimes. Once he appeared before the Committee, and his debt was paid to Lord Chester, Vincent meant to leave England and never look back.

Morning sunlight filtered through the grime on the lone bedroom window, making a mottled pattern upon the faded counterpane, but Janine would have ignored the light and sought to recapture her dreams were it not for a soft knock at her door.

"Yes," she called, her voice thick with sleep.

"Good morning," he said. "I have things to attend to in the stable, and will be out of the house for at least half an hour. The fire is going strong, so if you would like it, I can open your door and let some of the heat into your room."

Startled speechless by the novelty of someone sparing a moment's thought to her comfort, Janine was forced to swallow before she could manage a weak, "Thank you."

When the door opened, she yanked the cover close up under her chin, reminded that she wore nothing but a thin night rail. However, she need not have bothered with this little show of modesty, for her houseguest did not enter the room. All she saw of him was his hand, the long tapered fingers splayed against the dark wood of the door, pushing it all the way open until it thumped the wall.

Moments later she heard the kitchen door shut and knew she was alone in the house, alone for the first time since she had arrived. Now, with sunlight streaming through the window, revealing the truly disreputable state of the room, honesty compelled her to admit how grateful she was not to have been here by herself. She had enjoyed uninterrupted sleep last night—never once stirring—and she owed that peaceful slumber to Zach Flynn, to his presence in the next room.

Even though she had tried to make him leave the house—in deference to society's rigid rules regarding unchaperoned females—secretly she had been thankful that he had refused to go. Then he had totally confounded her by offering to share his food, and to place himself between her and possible intruders.

"Who are you, Zach Flynn? Certainly not the man I remember."

Janine shook her head, as if in so doing she might clear it of the many conflicting images inside her brain. Had she ever really known the man? With the identity of his father a mystery, everyone had branded Zach a bastard and expected him to act accordingly. Had he been the village bad boy merely to fulfill the expectations of the neighborhood? And his many escapades, were they nothing more than attempts to shock his detractors?

So many questions. And no answers. Janine was certain of only one thing, that no matter what Zach's reputation may have been in years past, last evening he had been both a good Samaritan and a gentleman.

As warmth from the kitchen permeated the bedchamber, Janine decided it was as good a time as any to rise and prepare for the day. She had plans to expedite and a long walk ahead of her.

Having settled upon a course of action, which was to throw herself upon Evangeline Craven's mercy until she could find a job, she knew there was no point in delaying the inevitable. Also, it behooved her to complete the task as early in the day as possible, for if by some chance the Craven sisters were from home, she would be obliged to devise another plan. Whatever the outcome, she did not wish to be caught by darkness once again.

Tossing back the cover and sitting up, Janine was surprised to discover that her rose merino dress no longer hung on the wall peg where she had left it, but was spread neatly across one of the chairs from the kitchen. Also, beside the chair stood her jean half boots, their surfaces scraped free of the mud that had clung to them when she removed them last night.

With a calmness that would have surprised her twenty-four hours ago, she walked over to the chair and touched the soft wool of the skirt. It was completely dry, all signs of yesterday's rain gone. Obviously the frock had spent several hours before the fire, and since Janine had yet to discover that clothing and chairs could move about unaided, she knew that Zach had entered her room.

Strangely, it did not embarrass her to think that he might have looked upon her while she slept—a reaction totally inconsistent with her having jerked the cover up to her neck only minutes ago. Actually, she was quite moved by his thoughtfulness in drying her clothes and cleaning her boots.

Determined to thank him for this, as well as for his kindness last evening, she donned the dress, then brushed her thick tresses until they shone, taking more time than usual in arranging her hair. Rather than pull it back severely, as Cousin Hortense had always insisted, she parted it in the middle and let the waves fall naturally in front of her ears. The remaining length she wound into a neat chignon which she secured at the nape of her neck.

Her toilette completed, Janine went in search of her knight errant.

Lifting her skirts, Janine tiptoed across the waterlogged stretch of land that had once been the kitchen garden, her destination the stable yard and the two-story brick rectangular building that comprised both the stable for the horses and a coach house capable of accommodating three vehicles.

When her parents had been alive, they had employed five servants. Of those five, only the females—the housekeeper and the two maids—had lived inside the house. The males—the coachman, who was also the gardener, and the lad-of-all-work—had occupied rooms above the coach house.

As she approached the building, she was surprised to see that it had withstood the years better than parts of the main house. The sun, shining in full springtime glory, revealed a sound roof and windowpanes that were filthy but still intact.

Once inside the stable portion, Janine paused to let her eyes adjust to the relative dimness. Breathing deeply, she fancied she smelled freshly turned hay and warm, well-brushed horseflesh, and the thought had no sooner occurred to her than it was confirmed by a soft whicker, the sound coming from the fifth of the six stalls. A man's bottle-green coat—of quality fabric, though no longer in style—lay folded across the open door of an adjacent stall.

"Comportate, por favor."

Surprised to hear words spoken in a foreign language—Spanish, she thought—Janine remained near the entrance, listening while Zach crooned incomprehensible phrases to the animal, almost as if they were conversing. A moment later she heard him laugh.

"Yes, Amigo, I know you are happy to see me, but I insist you not knock the bucket out of my hands. For such a well-bred animal, you display quite shocking manners."

When Zach began to whistle a haunting tune Janine had never heard before, she approached the stall quietly, enjoying the homey sounds of his whistling and the horse's dainty sips. As she drew near, the well-built chestnut lifted its beautiful head from the pail its owner held, and neighed a greeting.

"Oh," she said, "you are truly a magnificent animal."

"You are very kind," Vincent replied, not turning from his task, lest the horse bump the pail and spill water down his trousers. "I flatter myself that my face will not frighten young children, but I think to call me *magnificent* is coming it a bit strong."

He heard a quickly smothered laugh. "What a conceited jackass," she said.

"No. I assure you, Amigo is a horse."

"In this particular instance, Zach Flynn, I was referring to you."

Vincent sighed dramatically. "You certainly know how to hurt a fellow. And here I was thinking that your reason for entering this musty old stable on such a beautiful morning was to pay me a compliment."

"It is a lovely morning," she said, pointedly ignoring everything else. "After all that rain, the sight of the sun gives a person renewed hope that all one's problems can be solved."

Problems? So, she did have a reason for seeking him out.

In Vincent's somewhat checkered experience, when a young woman told a man she had problems, the confession generally cost the fellow a sizeable roll of flimsies. Familiar with the routine, he set the water bucket on the ground so he could give her his undivided attention. If Miss Morgan intended to try her hand at charming money from him, he did not wish to miss a minute of the performance.

Straightening, he turned toward her, and his first real look at her very nearly knocked him off his feet.

Deuce take it, I am a goner! Put in the well, with no one to toss me down a rope.

Vincent had suspected that Sir Burton's sister would clean up nicely, proving to be a fine-looking woman, but in this he had severely underestimated the case. The woman who stood before him was more than pretty. She was beautiful.

Her skin was the color of ivory—fine ivory, the kind used for carving delicate cameos—and so satiny he longed to reach out and touch it, just to see if it felt as smooth as it appeared. Her eyes were warm and alive as they looked at him, and the corners of her mouth were turned upward, the soft, full lips ready to smile.

Like her eyes, her hair was dark brown, and she had taken special pains with it, arranging it in a style that invited a man to slip his fingers beneath the thick waves in search of her pretty ears.

Of course, he already knew that she had beautiful hair. Late last night, when he had gone into her room to fetch her dress and take it to the fire, he had carried a spill with him. In the pale light, he had seen the silken tresses spread all over the pillow. They looked like nothing so much as a vat of melted chocolate that had just been tipped over, the rich syrup flowing deliciously in every direction.

At the sight, a lesser man might have been tempted to draw closer and have a taste. Vincent had withstood the temptation . . . but only just. Of course, her face had been turned away from him, and he had not yet seen her without the mud, a circumstance for which he now thanked heaven. If he had glimpsed that kissable mouth, the long night would have been even more miserable for him than it was.

Yes, he was definitely a goner. Whatever her problem, Vincent suspected he was about to pay dearly for the pleasure of making all right again. How could any man with blood in his veins possibly refuse a request from such a beautiful creature?

"You are in difficulty?" he said. "How may I be of service?"

The smile disappeared from her lips. "I did not say that *I* had a problem, merely that the sun gave *one* renewed hope that all problems might be solved."

Not a little surprised that she had ignored the opportunity to unburden herself, Vincent gave the gelding its oats, then stepped out of the stall, fastening both halves of the door behind him.

"Surely there is something that I may help you with, ma'am. Perhaps you are short of funds?"

Her ivory skin turned the color of a wild rose, and Vincent knew he had guessed correctly. She needed money. And since he had plenty, more than enough to share with an entire bevy of beautiful women, he was willing to expend some of it on her behalf. She need only ask.

"I have money," she informed him frostily, her back ramrod straight. "But even if I did not, what makes you think I would take any from you?"

Vincent was intrigued by the question, unaccustomed to having his offers refused. "You drank my tea, and ate my bread and cheese."

"Oh, that," she said, relaxing, "that was an entirely different matter."

"How so?"

"Because I . . ." She seemed to be searching for a logical explanation. "Because I shared my house with you!"

"I see. Then you accepted the food in lieu of rent."

For just a moment Vincent thought she meant to stiffen up on him again, but she surprised him instead by chuckling. It was an enchanting sound, low and throaty, reminding him of the soft, gentle call of the carrew, a small blue-winged parrot found along the backwaters of the Amazon River.

"You are being absurd again, Zach Flynn. I ate your food because I was hungry, and because you were kind enough to share with me. In fact, it was that generosity which brought me to the stable, for I wished to thank you. And," she added, extending her hand to him, "I wanted to tell you good-bye."

"Good-bye? Then you still wish to see me gone from the premises?"

Though he had no intention of leaving, Vincent took the hand she offered, closing his fingers around hers, enjoying the feel of her soft skin against his callused palm.

"I am not so ungrateful, sir. You obviously have some reason for wishing to remain here at Morgan House, and though I cannot think what it might be, if it is important to you, you may stay." She eased her hand from his. "It is I who will leave."

"You? But you only just got here. Where will you go?"

"To Dyrham Cottage."

She said the name as though expecting him to understand the significance of her removal there. "I see," he said, not wanting to blunder by saying too much. But concerned lest he was the cause of her removing from her home, he said, "And may I know why you feel you must go there?"

Initially her eyes flashed rebelliously at the impertinent question, but after a moment's reflection, she gave him an answer. "My purpose is quite simple. I hope to be invited to visit for a time, at least until I can find a post of some sort. I have no place else to go."

"But surely your brother will—"

"Ah, yes. My brother. When I believed Burton to be in residence here, I had planned to throw myself upon his mercy, to see if he would let me remain for a time at Morgan House. As you can see, that was but a dream. My brother has stripped the house of everything sellable, and from the looks of the place, he has no intention of returning. Since he has chosen not to inform me of his whereabouts, I can only assume that my welfare is of little importance to him."

Understandably, the earlier cheerfulness had disappeared from her voice, and Vincent added one more item to his list of scores to be settled with Sir Burton Morgan. "Is there no one to whom you may turn for help?"

Her eyebrows lifted in puzzlement at his question. "I just told you that I am going to the Misses Craven."

"Of course you did. I must have been woolgathering."

Vincent cursed himself for letting down his guard. She had mentioned only a place called Dyrham Cottage, but obviously the real Zach Flynn would have known of the connection between the Craven ladies and the cottage. "If I may be of service to you, I wish you would tell me."

"Wellll," she drawled, looking pointedly at the gelding who had finished his oats and was now watching them as if eavesdropping upon their conversation. "If you have some errand you wish to execute in the village, I would not refuse the offer of a ride to Miss Evangeline's."

"A ride? On Amigo?" He could only stare in dismay at the suggestion.

She nodded her head. "I have been away from the country for too long and am out of the habit of long walks. Furthermore, the lane will still be muddy, and since someone was thoughtful enough to clean my shoes, I should really hate to soil them again."

Vincent must have shown his misgivings about granting her request for a ride, for she suddenly laughed. "You act as if you had never seen me up behind Burton on that old bag of bones he had the audacity to call Julius Caesar."

It was not the idea of riding double that disturbed Vincent, it was the certain knowledge that she would expect Zach Flynn to know the way to Dyrham Cottage. Also, now that he knew the identity of the man he sought, he did not want to reveal himself to any villagers who might possibly warn Flynn away. Thinking fast, he said, "I, er, am not desirous of showing my face in the village. Not at the present time."

"Ah, yes. The truth finally comes out. What—or should I say who—are you hiding from?"

While Vincent searched frantically for a story that would satisfy her curiosity, she held up her hand to silence him.

"Please. It was impertinent of me to ask such a question. No matter what your reasons, you have a right to your privacy, so do not give it another thought. I shall walk."

She had already turned to leave when Vincent surprised himself by suggesting they compromise. "I could take you part of the way."

His suggestion was rewarded by a smile as soft as the May air. "Oh, thank you. I shall just run back to the house and get my bonnet."

While she suited the action to the words, Vincent fetched the saddle and tossed it onto Amigo's back, wondering as he did so why a man whose experience with women had left him if not suspicious, at least jaded, had jeopardized his plans just to please a female whose only repayment would be a smile.

"Sitting up all night must have left you fuzzy-headed," he muttered, tightening the cinch then reaching for the reins. "There could be no other explanation."

Chapter 4

Vincent slipped into the out-dated green coat he had thought suitable to wear as part of his disguise as a man of the road, and pulled a less-than-stylish hat down low on his forehead, hoping the brim and his thickening stubble would hide most of his face should anyone see him. With no way to rescind his offer of a ride, he led the gelding out into the sunshine, where he found Miss Morgan standing atop a mounting block. She had donned her pelisse and bonnet, and she held her valise in her hands.

"I am ready," she said cheerfully. "Actually, I feel quite daring, for I have not been on a horse in years."

Vincent was not immune to her unaffected manners and her willingness to view their riding together as an adventure, but he wondered if she had given the matter serious thought. A child sharing a horse with her youthful brother was not at all the same thing as a woman riding pillion with a man.

However, since it was not up to him to give instruction upon the subject of decorous conduct, he chose instead to comment upon her last statement. "It cannot be so very many years since you rode, for you are hardly more than a girl."

She made a derisive sound. "Do not waste your Spanish coin on me, Zach Flynn, for I am four and twenty, and well you know it."

"As old as all that?"

As he spoke, he swung up into the saddle, walked the horse to the mounting block, and reached for the valise. "I hope your ancient bones may not be too shaken up by the ride."

She threw him such a withering look that he was hard pressed not to laugh out loud.

"And *I* hope one day," she said, "to discover what misguided soul put out the story that you had a way with words."

"Alas, fair lady, I see you are determined to take exception to whatever I say. First you accuse me of offering you Spanish coin, then you berate me for speaking plainly. Is there no pleasing you?"

"You will please me by giving me your hand," she said. "For if the chestnut is ready, so are my ancient bones."

"Excellent. When I lean down," he instructed, "put your hands on my shoulders."

"But with Burton I always—"

"Humor me," he said. "You are no longer a girl, and I am not your brother."

There was a note of censure in his voice, and Janine was about to ask him to explain his words, when he leaned down and reached behind him, wrapping his arm around her and pulling her flush against him, as though he meant to carry her piggyback.

"Hands on my shoulders," he ordered.

Too rattled by the intimate contact to do otherwise, she obeyed, and immediately he straightened, lifting her with him until she was sitting sideways upon the gelding's haunches.

"All settled?"

Busy adjusting her skirt where it had flown up to reveal a goodly portion of her shins, Janine managed a rather breathless response, though her heart thumped so loudly she doubted he could hear the word. How truly he had spoken; this was not at all like her childhood gallops across the fields hanging on to her brother's coattail. This was a man and a woman on the same horse, their bodies so close she doubted a sheet of paper would fit between them.

The instant Zach had touched her, she knew she had made an error in judgment. Unfortunately, by then it was too late to cry off. Before she knew what was happening, he had wrapped his strong arm around her and lifted her off the ground. Once she was on the horse, she had no recourse but to settle herself behind Zach and get through the next three miles with as much dignity as possible.

"You might be more comfortable," he said, "if you put your arms around me."

A wave of heat rushed up from Janine's body and scorched her face. "This is just fine," she mumbled, pressing her hands down upon his shoulders.

"You may please yourself. But be warned, Amigo is a bit fresh. He may prove rather frisky for the first mile or so."

The accuracy of his words was confirmed before the gelding had left the stableyard, and in the few seconds it took the galloping horse to circle the house and reach the carriageway, Janine had abandoned her prim posture and slipped her arms around Zach's waist, clinging to him for dear life. Never mind that her bosom was pressed against his broad back; it was either endure the embarrassment of such close contact, or risk being thrown to the ground and trampled.

In accordance with the prediction, Amigo grew more manageable after the first mile. Thankfully, he settled into a gentle trot that allowed Janine to relax her death grip upon Zach's waist, though she dared not let go her hand long enough to straighten her bonnet.

"Are you still there?" he asked.

Detecting a hint of amusement in his voice, Janine was sorely tempted to give him a good punch in the ribs. "I warn you, sir, breathe but one *I told you so*, and I shall avail myself of that nasty looking knife that is but inches from my reach."

He laughed aloud. "Who would have thought that a mere twenty-four years was sufficient to make a female so bloodthirsty." Then, more gently, he added, "I would not have credited it in one who possesses such velvety soft eyes."

Because of Amigo's precipitous bolt down the carriageway, Janine was already having difficulty breathing; now, after Zach's unexpected compliment, her lungs seemed to cease functioning completely. And though she told herself that he was a practiced flirt, a man who left a string of broken hearts wherever he went, still his words caused a flutter within her ribcage that would not be denied.

Velvety soft eyes.

Too long deprived of kind words, Janine let the phrase warm her to the very soul, caring not at all that a true lady would have given him the setdown he so richly deserved. However, far from wishing to offer him a rebuff, she discovered within herself a feeling of tolerance—nay, receptiveness—toward other, similar, impertinences.

As it transpired, her forbearance was wasted, for the gentleman made no further comment, and within little more than a quarter of an hour, they reached the centuries-old stone bridge that crossed the swiftly moving brook. With the village within sight, he reined in the chestnut and reached back to assist her to alight.

This time, when he wound his arm around her, her brain did not register quite so much astonishment at the contact, though her heart was not nearly so sensible, accelerating its beat at an alarming rate.

"I wish you well," he said, handing her the valise. "And I thank you for allowing me to remain at Morgan House."

She took the valise, but overcome with a sudden unexplainable emptiness inside, she did not speak, merely nodded her head and turned away, walking at a quick pace. For a full minute, she heard nothing behind her; then, just at that precise moment when she could stand the silence no longer and turned to look at him, he made a clicking noise to the horse and galloped off in the direction from which they had come.

Dyrham Cottage was much as Janine remembered it. A two-story brick residence with four rooms and a kitchen below and six rooms above—two for the Misses Craven, and the remainder shared by the eight to ten boarding students who attended each year the Craven School for Young Females.

The dwelling boasted a heavy wooden door flanked by hawthorn bushes long since grown the size of trees, and leaded casement windows positioned at pleasing intervals on both floors. Built during Queen Elizabeth's reign, the cottage had been in the Craven family for most of its existence, the last owner before the two maiden sisters being their father, the Reverend Everett Craven.

Lovingly cared for and maintained, Dyrham Cottage was famed for its back garden, filled to overflowing with vegetables and herbs, as well as for its front garden, which was at the moment abloom with pink geraniums, yellow daffodils, white columbine, and purple foxglove and petunias, the whole encircled by scarlet pimpernel.

Whatever misgivings Janine entertained regarding her reception by the inhabitants, they were dispelled the instant the door was opened to her knock.

"Heaven bless me," the older of the Misses Craven said, stepping past the maid, Chloe, to embrace Janine in an exuberant hug. "Are you an illusion, child, or have you come in answer to my prayers?"

Janine had the grace to blush. "It is I who have been praying, Miss Evangeline. Beseeching heaven that you would not shut the door in my face, for I have been woefully remiss in not maintaining our correspondence."

"Pish and tosh," replied the tall, angular lady, adjusting the lace cap that threatened to slip off hair that was now more silver than light brown. "Come inside this minute so that I may have you to myself for a time. If we stand in the doorway much longer, every pokenose in the lane will invent some excuse to come calling, curious as to the identity of my guest."

After giving her former pupil a second, slightly less hearty hug, Miss Craven led the way to the breakfast parlor. "Perhaps we shall find a degree of privacy in here, my love, for you must know Edwina has taken over the withdrawing room for the express purpose of displaying her wedding gifts."

At the news, Janine's mouth fell open like the veriest widgeon's. "Wedding gifts? Miss Edwina? But—"

"Yes, I know," interrupted the bride's older sister. "Each morning I am greeted anew by the shock of it. On her next birthday, Edwina will be fifty years old— though she seems conveniently to have misplaced some half dozen of those birthdays—and here she is about to become a bride."

For the next few minutes, Miss Evangeline regaled her visitor with the high points of her sister's courtship with the new rector of St. Anne's. As for her future brother-in-law, a widower, she did not hesitate to stigmatize that gentleman as a bracket-faced slow-top whose self-proclaimed humility was as boring as it was justified.

"But his major flaw," she admitted with a shudder, "is his *worthiness*."

Unfortunately, Miss Edwina chanced to enter the room at just that moment, her still-blond sausage curls bouncing against her plump cheeks with each mincing step. Overhearing the final remark, she forsook her intended greeting to their visitor and delivered herself of a diatribe whose chief barb consisted of her sister's jealousy that she—the younger Miss Craven—was to be wed.

Once her anger was spent, the bride-to-be burst into tears and turned to quit the room. "You are consumed with envy," she said by way of a parting shot. "Jealous because no worthy gentleman has ever offered *you* his hand in holy matrimony."

"And just as well!" Miss Evangeline yelled at her retreating sibling, "for depend upon it, I should have thrown his offer back into his face. Give me a rogue any day!"

As Miss Edwina ran up the stairs, then down the short corridor to her bedchamber, the sound of her sobs grew fainter, and only after the betrothed lady slammed the door did Janine look at her friend.

"Do not say it," Miss Evangeline begged. "I know I behaved badly. The thing is, I cannot seem to stop myself. It would be best for both of us if I could take myself away for a fortnight, for since the students left last week, Edwina and I have done nothing but argue with one another."

She sighed, the sound filled with resignation. "If it were not for the unfelicitousness of May weddings, I would wish the ceremony tomorrow, so it could be done and over with."

"So you do not desire to put an impediment in the way of the marriage?"

The lady shook her head so vehemently the lace cap fell to her left shoulder. "Of course I do not. How could you even think it? You must know it would break Edwina's heart if anything were to prevent her from becoming Mrs. Worthy Slowtop."

Retrieving the cap, the lady began to laugh. "She is in the right of it, of course, about my being envious."

Janine smiled, happy to see that her old friend had lost none of her forthrightness. "You mean you would not, after all, prefer a rogue?"

"Oh, that part is true enough. When it comes to scoundrels, I am as silly as the next female. And if a rogue had ever offered for me, I assure you I would have been hard-pressed to say him nay. The truth of the matter is that no gentleman ever tossed the handkerchief my way—neither rogue nor worthy—and I suppose it is *that* circumstance which makes me tweak Edwina's nose at every opportunity."

"Are you saying you regret not having wed?"

"La! What a ridiculous idea, child. I never yet met a man I could abide for three hours in succession. As for taking one for the rest of my life . . ." She shuddered. "I merely regret not having been asked. If I had, just think of all the years I could have been throwing it in Edwina's face!"

Following a moment's stunned silence, Janine burst into laughter. Miss Evangeline, ever one to enjoy a good joke, even if it was at her own expense, joined in the fun, and only when her ancient tabby, Jezebel, came to investigate the noise did she regain her composure.

"Here, puss," she called, patting her lap in invitation.

The feline's topaz eyes filled with disdain at the suggestion she so demean herself as to do another's bidding. Turning her back upon the humans, she leaped onto the rounded arm of a wing chair and began to groom herself without further ado.

"I see Jezebel has not changed," Janine said.

"No, not at all. Like me, the old puss has vinegar in her veins, and is not the least bit affectionate. But she is the best mouser I ever had, so we tolerate one another."

Suddenly serious, Miss Craven folded her hands in her lap and gave her attention to her former pupil. "And now, my love, before I bore us both to distraction with a further cataloging of the foibles of the inhabitants of Dyrham Cottage, tell me what has brought you here. And spare me none of the details, for if I am to help you, I must know the whole."

Happy to unburden herself, Janine did as she was instructed, telling the entire story, beginning with her disappointment at discovering that her job as companion to her cousin was to be without remuneration, and finishing with the sorry state of Morgan House and the unexpected encounter with Zach Flynn.

"That rapscallion? What in heaven's name was he doing there?"

Janine shook her head. "I have no idea. I suspect he may be hiding from someone."

"Humph. Anything is possible with that one. But never mind him. It is you we must concentrate upon. Let me think for a moment."

Janine remained quiet for several minutes, her fingers laced together in nervous anticipation, allowing

Miss Craven ample time to come up with a possible solution to her problem. *She* had certainly thought of nothing constructive, and whatever her friend hit upon, Janine was determined to give it a try.

"I have it!" Miss Craven said, smiling happily. "Just the thing, for both of us."

"Oh, ma'am, tell me quickly, for I am beside myself with worry."

"Nothing easier. We shall return to Morgan House."

Chapter 5

It was as Janine remembered, once Miss Evangeline took hold of an idea, there was little short of flood, wind, or fire that would turn her from her chosen path.

"We shall do famously," her friend vowed. "All we need are provisions and a few linens."

"But—"

"Surely you see the wisdom of it."

"No, ma'am, I do not. In the first place, I told Zach Flynn that he could remain at Morgan House. And in the second, what about Miss Edwina? Surely you cannot mean to leave her when the wedding is a mere fortnight away?"

"I mean just that! It will afford me an opportunity to absent myself from the cottage, so that my sister may enjoy her prenuptials without constant doses of my vitriol. As for Zach," she continued with a snap of her fingers, "he shall not bother us. Furthermore, we might find him useful if we need a strong back to help us about the place."

"But I—"

"I am persuaded," she added, "that being at your home will allow you needed quiet in which to think through your career choices. At Dyrham Cottage all is chaos."

To every one of Janine's arguments, Miss Craven had a counter, even when the final piece of logic was presented. "You must believe me, ma'am, the place is totally uninhabitable. Not only is it indescribably filthy, but it is also overrun with mice."

Miss Evangeline merely smiled. "Do not give it another thought, my love." Reaching down her hand to wiggle her fingers enticingly upon the carpet, she called, "Here, Jezebel. Here, kitty, kitty."

Scheherazade, Miss Craven's pretty roan mare, trotted through the wrought-iron entrance gates to Morgan House, then up the carriageway, around the side of the house, and into the stableyard. The journey was all but completed, and Janine, sitting primly in the trap's divided seat, still could not remember actually agreeing to the scheme to return to her home.

While Miss Evangeline had bustled about, instructing her maid, Chloe, as to the number of linens she wished packed and the various foodstuffs she would require, her visitor had sat in the breakfast room watching the cat sharpen her claws upon the back of a yellow brocade settee. Within a very short time, the younger Miss Craven reentered the room, her earlier tears replaced by a smile of sweet relief.

"Thank you, dear child," she said, giving Janine a hug redolent of lemon verbena, "for taking my sister away. You must not think that I do not love her, for I do, but at this moment, I believe I shall love her better at a distance."

"But, I . . ."

Miss Edwina patted her cheek, as though she were still the little girl whose needlework was never quite as neat as that of her other students. "All will be well, my dear, I am certain of it. In the meantime, you may return Evangeline to me the first Sunday in June, but only just in time for the ceremony."

The bride-to-be's instructions being unanswerable,

Janine had remained quiet, a circumstance that prevailed during the entire three-mile drive back to Morgan House. Since all her arguments had fallen upon deaf ears, there was nothing to be done but let her friend see for herself just how ill-advised was this removal from Dyrham Cottage.

"The wagon and supplies should arrive within the hour," Miss Evangeline said, "for I can always depend upon Chloe to do what is needed in a timely fashion."

Pulling the mare to a stop just outside the stable door, she continued, "Until then, my love, where will I find that scamp, Zach Flynn? He can make himself useful by carrying this basket inside the house for us. Then, while you and I set out the nuncheon, he can see to Scheherazade."

Upon hearing the approach of the horse and trap, Vincent had ducked into the dimness of the stable. Now, after being privy to the lady's statement, and realizing that she meant to stay for a time, he stepped out into the light. He was once again in his shirt-sleeves, but he had chosen to don his hat, pulling the brim low over his forehead.

Aware of the intense scrutiny of the older lady in the no-nonsense chip-straw bonnet and the serviceable blue cloak, Vincent touched his finger to his hat brim in polite greeting.

"Miss Craven," he said, hoping he had guessed correctly, and that this woman with the nose that resembled a macaw's beak was indeed one of the inhabitants of Dyrham Cottage. "How nice to see you again, ma'am."

"Is it?" asked the lady. "I find that very interesting."

Somewhat taken aback, Vincent added, "If I may be permitted to say so, ma'am, you are looking as fine as fivepence."

The older lady nodded in acknowledgment of his compliment. "Of course, I am. It is my good fortune that gray hair and wrinkles are all the rage this season."

Vincent smothered a smile. "On you, ma'am, they are vastly becoming."

"Stuff and nonsense. Do give over with this flummery, sir, for I have a question that wants answering."

"I shall be happy to answer any of your questions. That is, if it is within my power to do so."

"Oh, it is," she assured him, looking from his partially concealed face to Janine's interested one. "Tell me," she said, "just who are you?"

Startled, Vincent schooled his countenance to show a calmness he was far from feeling. Trying a delaying tactic, he said, "I beg your pardon?"

The lady smiled. "You heard me right enough, young man. I would know who you are."

Miss Morgan gasped. "Miss Evangeline! The sunshine must have affected your eyesight. Surely you recognize Za—"

"My vision is perfect," she said, turning to her companion. "For that reason, my love, you may believe me when I tell you that this is the first time I have ever set eyes upon this young man."

"But, ma'am. You have known him all his life."

"No," she said, "I have not. I do not know who this person is, or what his game may be, but of one thing I am quite certain—he is not Zach Flynn."

Chapter 6

Vincent tried for a nonchalant air, though it was difficult with the iron-willed old lady staring down her macaw's-beak nose at him.

"Sir," she snapped, "you have not answered my question."

"Ma'am, I assure you—"

"Desist! I collect you are mindful to fob me off with some taradiddle, and if that is your purpose, allow me to inform you that it will not serve. I have known Zach since the day Rose Flynn delivered him, and though you look like the lad—the resemblance is quite uncanny, actually—you do not deceive me."

Vincent cursed silently. *Drat this woman with her parrot's nose and her hawk's eyes.*

"Speak up!" she admonished him. "For I have little patience with dissemblers."

"I can well believe it, ma'am. If I may hazard a guess, I would say that you have little patience with the human race in general."

"Not true, you impertinent young jackanapes. Though I do find that a disproportionate number of people vex me past endurance. Try, if you can, not to join their ranks."

"I shall make every effort," he said, offering her his hands to alight from the gig.

Miss Craven allowed him to help her down, but she did not give up her quest. "Thank you, Mr. . . . what shall I call you?"

"A fool, perhaps?"

"No," she said. Though she stood on the ground, and was obliged to look up at him, her steely-eyed examination missed nothing. "I may not know who or what you are, but I can see you are no fool."

He made her a slight bow. "Madam, you are too kind."

"What you are," she continued, as though he had not spoken, "is careless."

"Ma'am?"

"Before embarking upon this impersonation, you should have visited your barber."

Vincent rubbed his hand across his chin, the stubble making a rasping noise. "I apologize if my rough appearance offends you."

"Pshaw. I am not so easily offended, sir. But that is neither here nor there, for it is not your beard you should have removed; it is your hair."

Vincent resisted the temptation to touch the thick, jet black hair that brushed his shirt collar.

"Even with that hat on," Miss Craven continued, "I can see that you wear your hair rather longish. When I saw Zach scarce a month ago, his hair was quite short—*à la Titus*, I believe they call the style."

"Miss Evangeline," Miss Morgan said, "the thing one must remember about hair is that it grows. Faster on some, than on others. Surely you would not accuse a man of being a fraud simply because of the length of his hair?"

"No," she replied, "I would not do so. Not on that basis alone." Turning back to Vincent, she smiled. "You have remarkable eyes, young man. They are brown, are they not?"

"No, ma'am. With your—er—perfect vision, you must know that my eyes are gray."

"Very true. But I wished to hear the confirmation from your own lips. Obviously no one told you that Zach has amber eyes. 'Satan's own,' Rose Flynn was used to call them."

Satan's own. At the phrase, Vincent knew a moment's surprise.

Why had he not thought of that possibility before? With his father's propensity for pursuits of a more disreputable nature, it was more than likely that he had left by-blows scattered from one end of the kingdom to the other. Considering how much *he* looked like this father, it was altogether plausible that there might be others who bore a similar marked resemblance.

Who better than one of those by-blows to try his hand at the role of bogus baron?

Janine watched him run a practiced hand down the side of the roan's neck, seemingly unperturbed by Miss Evangeline's catechism. At no time did his countenance reflect anything more than a casual interest in the conversation.

"Well, sir," Miss Evangeline said, "what have you to say for yourself?"

He moved away from the horse. "I say it is time someone helped Miss Morgan down from the trap."

Suiting the action to the words, he walked around to the off side and held his arms up to her. "Allow me," he said.

Unsure what she should believe, Janine studied the man who stood before her, while at the same time trying to recall everything she could of Zach Flynn. Now that she pondered the subject, it seemed to her that she remembered Zach's good looks owing much to a ready smile and a well-formed face, the nose and chin beautifully chiseled, as if by the hand of a sculptor.

This man, though handsome by anyone's standards, possessed much more angular features, with an obstinate chin and a slight irregularity at the bridge of his nose where it had obviously been broken. Probably by someone's fist, Janine decided, for he was a man who confronted problems head on, ready to defend himself if need be. She knew, as surely as the sun rose each day, that he would never back down from a threat, nor seek to extricate himself by employing that willingness to charm that was so much a part of Zach Flynn.

So. He is a fraud.

Having admitted the truth of the situation, Janine was surprised to discover deep within her not a loathing for someone who had lied with the ease of practice, but a feeling of relief.

Only that morning she had questioned some of the inconsistencies between her memory of Zach and the actions of this man. She had been unable to reconcile the stranger's thoughtfulness with the self-interest that had always seemed to motivate the actions of her brother's friend.

"Ma'am?" he said, bringing her thoughts back to the moment and the arms he still held out to her.

Placing her hands on his shoulders, she allowed him to lift her down, and as he did so, he looked into her eyes. It seemed to Janine that those cool gray orbs asked a question of her.

Will you trust me? they asked. *Trust me, no matter what?*

The answer came to her without an instant's delay. She needed no time for contemplation, a circumstance that surprised her in view of the fact that she had every reason to distrust this stranger. He had misled her from the outset, and she had no idea who he was or why he wished to hide here at her home. Furthermore, he wore a deadly looking knife upon his person at all times—hardly a detail guaranteed to ensure confidence.

And yet, she trusted him, even more so now that she knew he was not Zach Flynn.

When her feet touched the ground, he did not release her, as she had expected, but continued to hold her, his strong, supple fingers pressing into the sensitive skin at her waist.

"Well?" he asked quietly.

Looking up into his face, she experienced a moment of light-headedness. "I . . . I am . . ."

"You are . . . ?" The words were softly spoken, a mere movement of his lips.

"I . . . I am hungry," she finally managed to say, the statement rushing willy-nilly from her mouth.

"Hungry?"

"Yes. Miss Craven has packed a hamper with all manner of delectable items. They . . ." she paused, unaccountably breathless, for his gray eyes still held hers, searching their depths. "They should prove a welcome addition to our bread and cheese."

"And bohea?"

She knew this spoken question had nothing whatever to do with tea, and that he awaited her answer to his silent plea for trust. "Yes," she said finally. "I trust you . . . as well as Miss Evangeline and I, will benefit from a cup of bohea. Will you get the hamper, please?"

"It will be my pleasure," he replied, the warmth in his smile dangerously impeding the work of Janine's lungs.

Lifting the hamper down, he looked across the trap at Miss Craven, who had eavesdropped unashamedly upon the exchange between her former pupil and the man who was *not* Zach Flynn.

"Ma'am," he said, giving the older woman a bow worthy of Almack's ballroom, "you have a discerning eye. And since you have found me out, I should be pleased if you would call me Vincent."

Janine knew her friend too well to be misled into thinking that she had abandoned all curiosity regarding Vincent. For that reason, Janine was not surprised to hear the subject introduced scarce half an hour later, when Miss Evangeline took a final sip from her cup and set the chipped crockery upon the scarred kitchen table, beside the equally chipped plate.

"Vincent," the lady said slowly, as though mulling over the name. "Is that Vincent *Something*, or Something Vincent?"

When he delayed his reply by studying a pattern of cuts and burns that had been etched into the table over the century or so it had stood in the kitchen, the lady continued. "I enjoy a conundrum as much as the next person, and for the most part I should be displeased if someone made me a present of the solution before I had an opportunity to work it out for myself. However, in this instance, I should like to be told the answer straight away."

"Forgive me, ma'am, if I seem obdurate, but for the moment, the conundrum must remain unsolved. You will oblige me, I pray, by contenting yourself with the one name."

Miss Craven raised an imperious eyebrow, appearing every inch the school mistress. "And what makes you think I have the least wish to oblige you, sir? Especially if by doing so I am remiss in my duty as Miss Morgan's friend? She has chosen to offer you the run of the house, and since I, too, am a guest, I cannot go against her wishes. However, if we are to reside *en famille*, as it were, it is incumbent upon us to know at least—"

Whatever information the lady felt they should know, it was not to be supplied at that moment. As one, they turned toward the open door, their attention caught by the sound of wagon wheels squeaking their protest as the blacksmith's hired vehicle lumbered into the stableyard. And though Janine was as curious as her friend to discover more of Vincent's identity, she was content, at least for the moment, just knowing that he was not Zach Flynn.

As it transpired, the inquisition was immediately forgotten, for even before the red-haired driver had pulled the large draft horse to a stop, Jezebel, Miss Evangeline's ancient tabby, strolled through the doorway, head and tail held high. Topaz eyes glanced from left to right, and though the feline tried to pretend indifference toward her new surroundings, a sudden stealthy movement near the larder door tempted her from her ennui and sent her in hot pursuit of an unwary intruder.

"Good girl," Miss Craven declared, watching the cat pounce upon the mouse. "Jezebel has seen fit to tackle her job without much ado, and I think it behooves the rest of us to do likewise."

Rising from the Windsor chair, she declared her intention of examining the servants' rooms to see which ones might be made habitable for herself and her maid. To Janine, she said, "Pray send Chloe to me straight away, my love." Then looking at Vincent, she continued, "As for you, sir, you may help young McFee with Janine's trunk."

"Yes, ma'am," he replied obediently, the quickly hidden smile not escaping the older lady's notice.

"Smile all you wish, sir, but a man cannot enter our circle shrouded in mystery—with only one name to his credit—and expect to be treated as though he were a duke in disguise."

This time Vincent laughed aloud. "Believe me, ma'am, I am no duke. Nor do I have the least desire to be treated as one." He made her a deep bow. "Furthermore, since hard work and I are old friends, you may consider me yours to command. The trunk, did you say?"

"Yes," Miss Evangeline replied, relenting so far as to nod in acknowledgment of his bow. The matter settled, she exited the kitchen, her destination the small bedrooms just past the larder. As for Vincent, he excused himself and went out to the stableyard.

Janine waited only until she had accomplished the task she had been given—directing the newly arrived Chloe to her mistress—then she hurried over to the door to observe the wagon driver's reaction to Vincent.

Would he be as quick as Miss Evangeline to realize that the person before him was not Zach Flynn?

The driver was a slender young man of perhaps twenty-two years, with an unruly thatch of red hair and an abundance of freckles splashed across his face, neck, and hands. Even if Miss Evangeline had not already called him by name, Janine would have had no difficulty in recognizing him as one of the numerous McFee offspring.

Because he was busy removing the trunk from the wagonbed, he did not hear Vincent approach, and when he turned around, he nearly let the heavy leather box slip from his shoulder.

"You!"

Being careful to keep his tell-tale gray eyes downcast, Vincent muttered something that must have passed for a greeting.

McFee adjusted his teetering burden, all the while glaring daggers at the man before him. "So this be where you've been hiding out. Happen Cal Aylesworth will be pleased to know the location of your hidey-hole."

"You think so?"

The homely face grew bright red with anger, making the freckles appear even more pronounced. "I know so. And it wouldn't surprise me none if Cal was to come calling on you real soon." A sneer pulled at his thin lips. "No, it wouldn't surprise me at all, seeing as how he weren't best pleased to come home with a bullet hole in his arm."

Janine gasped to hear that the blacksmith's son had been shot. Normally she would have been sympathetic toward anyone so injured, but in this instance she was much more disturbed by the identity of the wounded person, and the suggestion that he might wish to wreak vengeance upon Vincent for the mishap.

She remembered Cal Aylesworth quite well. About her own age, the older of the blacksmith's two children was a giant, with the physical strength of two men, and the intractability of a loaded cannon running downhill. The quality that made him most dangerous—the one that had earned him his reputation as the neighborhood bully—was his tendency to blame others for any misfortune that befell him. Once he settled upon his choice of supposed culprit, he pursued him relentlessly, until he made him pay the price for his alleged crime.

Cal had always treated Janine with grudging deference, but she suspected even that show of civility had less to do with the fact that she was a female and more to do with her being the daughter of a respected gentleman. Unfortunately, her brother's experience with the fellow had not been quite so convivial. In fact, she recalled several times when Burton went so far as to cross the street to avoid passing too close to the blacksmith shop.

Unaware of how much, or how little, Vincent knew of the townspeople in general, and the Aylesworths in particular, Janine felt she must warn him of the possible danger.

McFee spat upon the ground, the gesture one of contempt. "I warned the lads not to pay you no heed. I knew how it would be. 'Don't listen,' I told 'em. 'The bastard's full of wild schemes and glib talk, and spouting the same kind of empty promises to you boys that he uses on all the females.' "

The angry driver muttered an oath. "Not that any of 'em listened to a word I said. No more than Franny did when I begged her to cast you from her heart and give it to one who would revere—" He stopped short, apparently angry with himself for revealing more than he had intended.

After a moment's awkward silence, he would have pushed past Vincent, but the larger man stepped in front of him, blocking his path.

"How did Aylesworth get shot?" Vincent asked. "What happened?"

"What happened? You may well ask."

Leaning forward, he set the trunk on the ground. "That coach driver you said would give over . . . well, he didn't. The lads jumped from behind the hedge and shouted for the yahoo to halt, just like you told 'em to, but instead of doing like they said, he pulled out his barkers. Opened fire, he did, winging Cal just above the elbow."

McFee's hands clenched into fists, and he looked as

though he contemplated trying his luck at drawing Vincent's cork. "Cal is hurt, and it's your doing, Zach Flynn. Same as if you had took the pistol to him yourself."

Wisely keeping his hands at his side, the redhead contented himself with calling Vincent a truly vile name. The larger man did not even blink, and Janine marveled that he let the insult pass.

"It were just like I foretold," McFee continued, emboldened by having gotten away with the vile epithet. "I warned 'em you'd disappear when it came to the sticking point. And disappear you did. You was supposed to be back here night before last to lead 'em. Where were you, boy-oh?"

"I was delayed." Vincent replied quietly.

"Delayed? Of all the lame, idiotic excuses I ever heard, that be the worse. Did you think the full moon would wait upon your pleasure?" He spat again. "Course you did. Not but what it be just like you to go planning something as risky as a robbery, then taking yourself off and leaving the doing of it to a bunch of lads what know nothing save plowing and haying."

Janine's heart nearly stopped. *Great heavens! He was talking about highway robbery!*

Vincent still did not look directly at the driver. "How is Cal?"

"How do you think he be? How'd you feel if a ball passed through your arm?"

The questions were obviously rhetorical, for McFee did not give Vincent time to answer; instead, he laughed, the sound short-lived and without humor. "Course, once Cal Aylesworth gets through with you, you may be wishing it'd been you what took that piece of lead instead of him."

He bent and retrieved the trunk, hoisting it once again upon his shoulder. "Only wish I could be there to see him give you what for. Wish Franny could witness it too. I know you'll prove a coward, Flynn, and happen once she sees your true colors, she'll stop mooning over you and settle down with a fellow what will treat her right."

Having said his piece, the young man edged past Vincent and strode toward the kitchen door.

Janine waited only long enough to point McFee toward the housekeeper's bedchamber, advising him in a composed manner to set the box on the floor just inside the room. However, as soon as he quit the kitchen and was out of sight, she abandoned all pretence of calm. Desirous of informing Vincent with all due haste that he must not, under any circumstances, confront Cal Aylesworth, she lifted her skirts above her ankles and ran out to the stableyard.

Cal was a dangerous man, and Vincent must be made to understand that fact. And while she had his ear, Janine meant to try what she could to convince him to give over this impersonation of Zach Flynn. No matter what his reasons for the subterfuge, they could not be important enough to risk serious injury.

For his part, Vincent was not disturbed in the least by the threat of a possible altercation with the local bully, for he had met many such men, both in the jungles of South America and in the so-called civilized world. What concerned him was the discovery that he had walked into a situation even more complicated than he had expected. It seemed his father's by-blow was involved in more than just that dirty business in town.

Not content with passing himself off as a peer and bilking several members of the *ton*, the bogus baron had masterminded a plan for highway robbery that involved a number of naive country lads. And though it was the former circumstance that had brought Vincent into East Sussex, it was the latter that boded ill for his chances of accomplishing his mission of apprehending Flynn unhindered.

If Vincent succeeded in hauling Flynn back to London to stand trial for the beating of young Mr. Neville, the rascal might well attempt to save himself by giving evidence against this bunch of plowboys. It was a logical assumption, for any man who would beat a callow youth within an inch of his life would think nothing of exposing a few of the local lads to prosecution for attempted robbery.

And if *Vincent* recognized this possibility, so would the lads.

Therein lay his principal concern. If he tried to take Flynn in, would he find himself facing a mob comprised of men from half a dozen families in the neighborhood? Such men would be prepared to fight. Not for Zach Flynn's sake, of course, but for the protection of their misguided sons and brothers.

With this possibility weighing upon his thoughts, Vincent entered the stable and walked over to the stall where he had placed Miss Craven's roan mare slightly more than an hour ago. The animal should be dry by now and ready to be brushed free of the mud she had acquired on the trip from the village.

Knowing how physical labor always helped him think through a problem, he brought Scheherazade to the center of the stable and fastened her between two posts, where he had ample room in which to work at grooming her stomach and flanks.

With a currycomb in his right hand, he worked in a circular motion, loosening the mud; then, with his left hand slipped through the leather loop of a brush, he whisked away the offending dirt. Taking long, gentle strokes he groomed Scheherazade, while the roan stood quietly, like the lady she was, allowing him to minister to her needs.

He whistled as he worked, as much to clear his own thoughts as to calm the mare, and because of the sound, he did not hear Miss Morgan until she was within a few feet of him. She stopped quite near Scheherazade, reaching out to touch the snow-white blaze on the mare's forelock.

One look was sufficient to convince Vincent that this was no casual visit, for Miss Morgan's breathing was audible, as though she had run the distance from the house to the stable, and her dark brown eyes were bright with concern.

"What is amiss?" he asked.

"Oh, nothing," she replied, though she did not look directly at him.

"Something has cut up your peace. Will you not tell me what it is?"

She did not answer right away, and when she did, the words surprised him. " 'Tis you," she said, "who has me concerned."

"Me? If I have done something to upset you, Miss Morgan, I beg you will forgive me. Though, in all honesty, I cannot think what—"

"It is not so much what you *have* done, but more what you might do."

"Which is?"

She sighed, as though exasperated. "Men are such illogical creatures, there is never any knowing what they may do. But whatever it is, I am persuaded I will not like it."

He was tempted to laugh, amused at this piece of feminine logic, but the serious look upon her face kept him silent.

"And," she said, as though this new statement was

a continuation of the first, "I am furious with Zach Flynn, for he has put you in serious jeopardy."

Vincent stepped away from the mare. After tossing the currycomb and brush onto the stable floor, he bent and dipped his hands into the pail of water he had set there earlier. He took his time working the crude bar soap into a lather, for he needed a moment to absorb the rather novel idea that anyone should actually be concerned for his welfare. As he reached for the drying cloth, he said, "What makes you believe me to be in jeopardy?"

"I know Cal Aylesworth. I know what he is capable of, and . . ." she paused for a moment, "and I am frightened for your safety."

The words had been uttered reluctantly, as though she were torn between the need to warn him and a wish not to insult his masculine pride. Vincent found the idea oddly touching.

"You need not be frightened for my sake, you know."

"But I am. I just wish I had Zach Flynn here this minute. I would gladly wring his neck!"

This time Vincent chuckled. "There is that bloodthirsty streak again. I wonder that the redoubtable Miss Craven did not see fit to expunge such violent tendencies from her pupils."

A smile fought with the angry set of Miss Morgan's face, making the corners of her mouth quiver. Finding himself unaccountably charmed by the sight, Vincent knew a momentary desire to feel the softness of her lips, to cover her mouth with his and taste the sweet nectar of her kiss.

"I see what you are thinking, sir."

At the provocative remark, he looked into her eyes. Detecting not a hint of guile or coquetry, however, he said, "No, madam, I do not believe you do. Else you would be threatening me with all manner of barbarous acts."

This time the smile would not be denied, and Vincent was treated to a glimpse of a dimple in her right cheek. "I collect, sir, that you are making sport of me."

"Only just a little."

"Well I wish you would not, for I am in earnest."

"I can see that," he replied quietly.

"I know you will be thinking me a veritable pokenose, but my conscience will not let me remain silent while you walk into a situation so fraught with danger. Cal Aylesworth is a formidable fellow, with limited reasoning power, and he will be seeking revenge for his injury. For that reason, if for no other, you should not have encouraged McFee to continue in his belief that you are Zach Flynn."

While she spoke, Vincent used the drying cloth to brush a layer of dust from the top of an oat barrel. "Please," he said, "will you not be seated?"

When she accepted his invitation, but found the barrel too high to climb upon, he placed his hands on either side of her waist and lifted her onto the makeshift chair.

As his fingers encountered the delicate bones beneath the slim waist, he was struck by the incongruity of this young woman—of her slender frame and her stalwart inner strength. She was alone in the world, with no one to stand between her and the harshness of life, yet she was concerned for *his* sake, worried that he might bear the enmity meant for Zach Flynn.

If she only knew it, it was she who needed protection. From him!

Standing so close to her, Vincent was obliged to battle an almost overpowering urge to slip his arms around her and draw her near. And he was honest enough to admit it was not her inner strength he wished to mold against his chest. It was her tantalizing, womanly softness.

Not unlike Vincent, Janine found their closeness unnerving. Her senses reeled from the ease with which he had lifted her, and as she sat quite still, watching his face, a look darkened his gray eyes—a look that made it difficult for her to breathe.

Though she had spent the last three years with little or no contact with members of the opposite sex, she was woman enough to know *that* look in a man's eyes. He wanted to kiss her. And if the intense pounding beneath her ribs was anything to judge by, she was not averse to the idea.

As a matter of fact, she was having a difficult time schooling her traitorous body, for it wanted desperately to sway toward Vincent, to feel the strength of his arms and the hardness of his chest.

"How did you know that I encouraged McFee to believe I was Zach Flynn?"

"What?" she asked, startled to hear such a mundane question when she had expected to be kissed.

Vincent stepped back, letting his hands fall to his sides, and Janine felt the loss of his warmth. If he felt a similar loss, it was not evident in his expression, for he was once again the smiling, congenial man he had been earlier when they had shared Miss Evangeline's picnic hamper.

How could he appear so unmoved? Had she been mistaken about his wanting to kiss her? Perhaps the wish had been hers alone. It was a lowering thought.

"You accused me of encouraging young McFee to believe I was Flynn. How could you have known that?"

Still too disappointed to guard her tongue, she said, "I eavesdropped."

"Did you, now?" He spoke softly, but there was a slight teasing tone in his voice. "That answers a question that has been on my mind since I saw you first thing today."

Not if her life depended upon it could Janine have ignored that intriguing non sequitur. "A question? About me?"

"About your ears, actually."

He reached toward her, his finger lightly skimming the thickness of hair that was draped loosely over her ears, leaving only the very tips of the lobes exposed. At his feathery touch, a delicious shiver coursed along her spine.

"I was wondering if the thickness of your tresses ever interfered with your hearing."

"No," she said, albeit breathlessly, "never."

She could have told him that her hair did not hinder her hearing nearly as much as his closeness impeded her breathing, but before she could reveal that fact, he drew his hand away and walked over to the mare, reclaiming the currycomb and brush and resuming the task he had abandoned.

"While you were eavesdropping," he said, "I suppose you heard what McFee said about the attempted robbery."

She nodded her head. "I did. Though I find such dishonorable behavior difficult to believe, even of Zach Flynn. Nor can I credit his thoughtlessness in dragging some of the local lads into his scheme."

For a moment she remained silent, for thoughts of the attempted robbery put her in mind once again of Cal Aylesworth. "I hope you heed my warning about Cal. He is not a man to take lightly."

Vincent paused in his task long enough to look directly at her. "I try always to treat the unknown with a degree of respect. Besides, from the amount of pleasure McFee derived from informing me of Aylesworth's anger, I assumed the fellow must be rather prepossessing."

"Prepossessing? The word does not begin to convey the whole, for Cal is as big as a mountain!"

Vincent lifted one eyebrow. "As big as all that?"

"Bigger."

From the smile lurking in his eyes, Janine could not be certain if he took her seriously, but at least she had warned him.

"The driver also mentioned someone named Franny. Who is she?"

"Franny Aylesworth," Janine replied offhandedly, not altogether pleased to have a new topic introduced. "She is the blacksmith's daughter. And Cal's sister, I might add."

Apparently ignoring her attempt to reintroduce the subject of his possible nemesis, Vincent continued to speak of the sister. "From the sound of McFee's voice when he spoke the girl's name, I gather he is in love with her."

"I should not be at all surprised. When I left Bexham three years ago, every male between the ages of nine and ninety was mad for her."

"You don't say? She's a comely lass then, is Miss Franny?"

Knowing he was trying to tease her into changing the focus of her conversation, Janine tried to stick to her purpose, but when he smiled, she found it difficult not to respond in a like manner. "I suppose one might say Franny is attractive. Especially if one admires hair that is both long and silken, and the color of golden wheat swaying in the soft morning air. Or if one has a fondness for eyes as green as the leaves of the wood sorrel."

Vincent whistled in amazement. "Definitely comely! And her figure? What might one say of that?"

"Oh, only that it is pure perfection. And, should you be interested in such things, I have heard it said that Franny is an accomplished dancer. Every bit as graceful as—"

"Please," he said, holding up his hand for silence. "Say no more, for I am halfway to falling in love with the damsel myself. And that would never do."

"It would not?" Janine asked, inordinately pleased by the information, and hoping, illogically, that he might mention a preference for ladies with somewhat darker hair and eyes.

"Of course it would not. For then I should have both 'The Mountain' and young McFee wishing to put a period to my existence."

Before she could reply to this piece of truth-in-jest, her attention was claimed by the sound of someone approaching the stable. From the masculine footfalls, it could not be Chloe or Miss Craven, and Janine was certain she had heard McFee drive away several moments earlier.

Curious as to who else would be calling, she stared at the arched doorway where afternoon sunlight cast a softly defused glow all around the opening. Into this eerie light stepped an ethereal being seemingly lifted directly from one of Michelangelo's canvases.

Her tongue momentarily stolen by the appearance of such an apparition, Janine watched as the being strode from the light into the relative dimness of the stable, thereby transmogrifying into a creature of this earth.

"Sir," she said, happy to regain her powers of speech, "what a start you gave me."

"Your pardon, ma'am."

The slender young gentleman turned toward the

sound of her voice, removing his hat as he did so. "Forgive me for coming around unannounced, but I gave up hope of anyone ever answering the front door. I must have knocked for a full ten minutes."

"Then it is I who should beg your pardon, sir, for the lack of hospitality. But if you are looking for my brother, I must tell you that he is not here. Nor has he been in residence for some time."

"Oh, no, ma'am," he said, peering into the depths of the building and blinking as if to help his eyes adjust to the change in light. "I do not want your brother. What I mean to say, I do not know who that may be, so why would I be looking for him?"

"An interesting point, sir. However, if you are not here in search of Sir Burton, perhaps you are come to the wrong place."

The gentleman's mouth fell open. "Your brother is Sir Burton? Sir Burton *Morgan*?"

"That is correct. I am Miss Morgan."

Appearing decidedly ill-at-ease, the visitor began to back out of the stable. "No wish to disturb you, ma'am. It would appear that I am, indeed, in the wrong place."

"That is an understatement," Vincent said, stepping from beside the mare.

Suddenly all smiles, the young man halted his backward steps. "Thank's be," he said.

Obviously unable to discern the scowl on his quarry's face, he extended his hand. "Cousin Vincent! How glad I am to have found you."

Chapter 7

Vincent only just stopped himself from uttering a most indelicate word—one totally unfit for the ears of a gently reared female. Instead, he strode directly to the door, covering the distance in a half dozen long, angry strides, halting in front of the handsome youth. His voice just above a whisper, he muttered through tight lips, "What the deuce are you doing here? I distinctly remember putting you on a stagecoach bound for Hereford and my Aunt Letitia."

"Cousin, I—"

"No! Do not say another word. Not here."

"But I—"

"Silence."

Recalling that Miss Morgan was a self-confessed eavesdropper, he took the young man by the arm and ushered him none too gently from the stable, not stopping until they reached a copse of beech trees some distance away. "And now," he said, "why the deuce are you here? And the truth, mind you. I am not the bagwig, so spin me no schoolboy yarns."

"No, sir. I will not do so. It is just . . ."

"Just what? Speak up, lad. These past two months have fallen sadly short of the homecoming I had envisioned, and as a result, my patience is wearing dangerously thin."

"I know, cousin. That is why I am here. I . . . I have come to help."

"To help! What in blazes do you think you can—" He curbed his tongue, suddenly realizing how close he had come to letting his anger get the better of him.

Gareth was still a lad, never mind that he was up at Cambridge, and no one knew better than Vincent how damaging an ill-advised remark could be, or how long a disparaging comment could eat away at a youngster's feelings of self-worth. Years after he had put away the memories of the severe physical chastisement meted out by his father—punishment that far exceeded the boyish crimes—the remembered mental abuse had still possessed power to undermine Vincent's confidence.

He might still be battling that particular demon if it were not for the intervention of Lord Chester.

Recalling his mentor, the man who had saved him from the bitterness that was governing his life, Vincent grew calm. Lord Chester had discovered an angry boy working in the sugarcane fields of Barbados, and he had take that youth under his wing, becoming the father Vincent had always longed for. In his quiet, unassuming way, the gentle botanist had shown Vincent how all living things were of value, both to themselves and to the world.

Ten years they had traveled the Amazon together— Vincent and his adopted father—with Lord Chester sketching and cataloging the thousands of plants indigenous to the nearly four-thousand-mile river, and Vincent standing watch, keeping them both safe from the many predators of the jungle.

It was for Lord Chester's sake that Vincent had finally returned to England. It was for the sake of Lord Chester's work that he needed a reputation free of blemish.

"I . . . I'll do anything you say, cousin. If you will only let me help you."

Called back to the present by Gareth's quiet plea, Vincent released the lad's arm. "Perhaps you can be of service to me," he said, the anger gone from his voice. "But first you must promise me two things."

"Anything. You have but to name it."

"Good lad," he said, placing his hand on Gareth's shoulder. "I knew I could count on you."

Trying not to notice the hero worship that shone in the deceptively angelic blue eyes, Vincent extracted his promise. "First, you must post a letter to your parents informing them that you are with me. And second, you must give me your solemn oath to do only what I tell you. Reputations, and possibly lives, are at stake here, and as in the jungle, a careless disregard for orders could prove disastrous."

Gareth squared his shoulders. "You have my word, sir."

Having pledged his allegiance to his cousin, and receiving a firm handclasp to seal the bargain, Gareth plied him with questions. "Have you found the blackguard who is impersonating you? The one who beat Mr. Neville and left him for dead?"

"Not yet."

"But that is why you are here at Morgan House, is it not? To find Sir Burton and his despicable crony, so you can take them back to town to stand trial for the near murder?"

At the last question, Vincent heard a quickly smothered gasp, the sound coming from behind a large beech tree at the edge of the copse. Though he cursed himself for his gullibility in not expecting something of the sort, he ignored the eavesdropper for the moment. "How did you get here?" he asked his young cousin.

"I traveled to Bexham by stagecoach."

"I meant how did you get to Morgan House."

"By hired hack. When I discovered that the estate was several miles outside the village, I hired a horse at the blacksmith's shop." After making a derisive sound, he added, "Although how the smithy had the nerve to call that vile-tempered collection of bad points a horse, is more than I can say. You would not believe how the brute—"

"Where is the animal now?" Vincent asked, not wanting to engage in a discussion of horseflesh.

"I left him tied to a trellis arch at the front door."

"Go fetch him."

Once the lad was safely out of the way, Vincent approached the edge of the copse, stopping several feet from the concealing beech tree. With only a hint of censure in his voice, he said, "In this instance, Miss Morgan, I wish you had not let your curiosity get the better of you."

When he spoke her name, she stepped from behind the tree, obviously too shocked by what she had overheard to care that she had been caught in a reprehensible act. Though her face was unusually pale, her dark eyes looked daggers at him.

"It is not true," she said. "My brother is not a murderer."

"I sincerely regret that you heard that."

"Oh, I wager you do. Otherwise, you could have continued to reside here at Morgan House, abusing Burton's hospitality and making a fool of me, all the while trying to prove my brother a murderer!"

For two reasons, Vincent did not try to deny the accusation. First, the lady was too angry to listen, and second, there was enough truth in what she said to make the whole unanswerable.

"Since you were obviously not privy to my entire conversation, ma'am, allow me to put the record straight. The young man was not killed, merely injured."

"That he lives is, indeed, good news, but the fact remains that no matter what the gentleman's misfortune, Burton had nothing to do with it."

"Believe me, Miss Morgan, I admire your loyalty, but at the same time, I wonder how you can be so certain? If I remember correctly, you told me that you had not seen or heard from your brother in more than three years."

"That is true, but . . ."

She fell silent, and Vincent watched a myriad of emotions reflected in her eyes. He could see that her basic honesty was fighting with what remained of her righteous indignation.

"I . . . I will admit that my brother is spoiled, and perhaps not as considerate as he might be." The words had been spoken softly, reluctantly, and almost immediately she squared her shoulders, as if daring Vincent to comment. "But you may believe me when I tell you that Burton would never inflict bodily harm upon another human being. He is no more capable of such a cowardly act than am I. You . . . you have mistaken the matter, sir."

"I hope that may be the case," Vincent replied quietly. "For your sake. I have no wish to bring you pain."

Not immune to the gently spoken words, Janine looked into his eyes. Deep within those gray orbs she saw regret, but she saw something else there as well—truth. She might not like what Vincent had said about her brother, and she was definitely angry with him for not telling her right away why he had come to her home, but she could not deny that *he* believed what he said was true.

Relenting somewhat, she said, "Leaving out the

part about my brother, is the remainder of what your cousin said accurate? The part about someone impersonating you?"

"It is."

"Was it Zach Flynn?"

"Perhaps. I cannot say for certain. Someone—it might have been Flynn—has been using my name to gain admission to certain gaming establishments where the play is deep. For a time he was uncommonly lucky, winning night after night; until young Neville accused him of being a bit *too* lucky. That same night, Mr. Neville was savagely beaten."

"But that could have been just an unfortunate coincidence. Surely you know what a dangerous city London is. People are accosted there with frightening regularity."

"True. But the young man's grandfather does not believe it was an act of random violence. Furthermore, he believes that *I* was the assailant."

"What! How could he believe such a thing?"

"Quite easily. Especially since it was my face—or, rather, one bearing a strong resemblance to my face—that witnesses claim to have seen close to the scene of the crime."

"But you would not have done something so reprehensible."

He made her a bow. "I appreciate your vote of confidence, but others are convinced of my guilt. To disabuse them of their conviction, I must produce the person who pretended to be me."

Janine sighed. "So, we have come full circle, and are back to Zach Flynn."

"I am afraid so. And if it was Flynn who committed the crime, and I can find proof of his involvement, I intend to see he stands trial."

"And Burton?"

He shrugged, and though his eyes were filled with regret, his posture said he would not be swayed from his resolve. "You said yourself that your brother and Flynn were friends of long standing. And according to several reliable sources, Sir Burton and the imposter were seen together in town quite recently. Of course," he added softly, "the witnesses could be mistaken."

"They are," she said, though she wished with all her heart that she had more faith in her own assertion. "And I will prove it."

Janine lay upon her bed, the smell of clean, fresh sheets sweet in her nostrils. While she had been absent from the house, Chloe had been busy making the three small bedchambers habitable. Like one possessed, the maid had turned mattresses, swept away years of dust and cobwebs, and scrubbed the floors until they shone. Even now Janine could hear her in the kitchen, emptying drawers and shelves, blessing herself at the unbelievable filth, and splashing water about as she put the room to rights.

However, the straightening of the house was of little importance to Janine, for she could think of nothing but what she had overheard. It was true what was said of eavesdroppers, for they did, indeed, hear ill of themselves; or, as in this instance, of some family member. With the wisdom of hindsight, she wished she had remained in the stable.

But of what good was ignorance? She would have learned the truth sooner or later, and been obliged to face it. Vincent needed proof of his innocence, and under normal circumstances she would have offered to help him find it, if she could. Unfortunately, in this instance she had a more pressing need—to prove that his suspicions about her brother's complicity in a violent crime were unfounded.

She had lain upon the bed for the better part of an hour, racking her brain for some plan that would enable her to prove Burton innocent of any wrongdoing. So far, it had been an exercise in futility. She had gained nothing from her mental exertions but a mussed bed, a sadly rumpled dress, and the beginnings of a pounding headache.

Not even a glimmer of an idea had come to her about where to begin to search for the truth. In this, she supposed, she and Vincent were on equal footing, for he had followed his one clue to Morgan House, and was now trying to discover some new piece of information that would put him on the right trail. All he had learned so far was that given the right circumstances, he and Zach Flynn were indistinguishable.

And *she* had told him that!

It was while Janine reviewed everything she knew of the village bad boy that a plan began to take shape in her brain. Vincent wanted information to prove that Zach and Burton were guilty of the beating of young Mr. Neville, while she needed similar information to establish her brother's innocence. Simple logic told her that the two investigations must lead them in the same direction.

Could they not pool their efforts?

Of course they could! In fact, it was probably the only way either of them would succeed.

Her headache miraculously banished, Janine sat up and swung her legs over the side of the bed, eager to find Vincent and tell him of her plan. He would agree to their working together—she was convinced of that fact—for he was far too intelligent to let such an excellent opportunity slip through his fingers.

After all, *she* had been born and reared in Bexham; she knew the area and the people. Furthermore, no one would wonder at her asking questions about her absent brother, or about his friend, Zach Flynn.

On the other hand, Vincent was a stranger in a village where the locals considered anyone an outsider whose family had not lived in the neighborhood for at least fifty years. And as an outsider, he would be suspect. Of course, he might try to pass himself off as Zach, but after the fiasco of the attempted robbery, there was every likelihood that the villagers would shoot first and answer his questions later.

Hurrying across the room to the trunk McFee had brought from town, Janine pulled out a simple frock of jonquil yellow muslin—a dress her looking glass told her complimented her dark hair and eyes. She donned the frock, then twitched the skirt into place, adjusting the amber satin ribbon that tied beneath her bosom then hung down almost to the hem. "My plan will work," she said, "but it might be wise to look as neat as possible. Especially since Vincent has never seen me in anything but that crumpled old traveling dress."

Ten minutes later, as Janine crossed the kitchen garden on her way to the stableyard, she saw Vincent standing in the arched doorway, watching her approach. He appeared so tall, so formidable, and so completely self-reliant, seemingly unafraid of anyone or anything. Such a complex man.

Doubly glad she had put on the jonquil frock and dabbed a drop of lilac water behind each ear, Janine tried to pretend she did not see him standing there. It was pure pretence, of course, for she knew he watched her every move, and she would wager her last groat that he knew she knew.

As she drew near, she fancied she could feel his thoughts—they were of her, and of the fact that he and she were on opposite sides of a dilemma. Had she not been pondering that same problem just minutes ago? And had she not been miserable thinking that she and Vincent would be working against one another?

Now, of course, she felt immeasurably better, for she knew they could work together. And once Vincent saw the beauty and simplicity of her plan, she was certain he would be unable to say her nay.

"Absolutely not!" he said.

"But, Vincent, can you not see the wisdom of our joining forces?"

"Can *you* not see that you would be at risk?"

"Fustian! What harm could come to me?"

"None at all," he said, "for you will stay out of the business. Now, please, let us speak no more about it."

"But you need me. You will waste precious time just finding your way around the village."

"In that, Miss Morgan, you are quite mistaken. I need no one. I made it through the wilds of South America without a guide, and I flatter myself that it will not prove too taxing to navigate one small English village."

"Perhaps," she added airily, "but if you mean to assume Zach Flynn's identity, you will need to know the best places to duck behind the hedgerows."

"I beg your pardon?"

"You will need hiding places."

"Oh? And why is that?"

"Jealous husbands," she replied smugly.

After a moment of surprised silence, Vincent gave vent to a hearty laugh. "Allow me to inform you, madam, that you are a saucy minx."

As if taking it for a compliment, she executed a curtsy deep enough for the most formal of occasions, though she ruined the effect by gazing up at him and feverishly batting her eyelashes. "La, sir. You are too kind."

"Thoroughly saucy," he said, taking her hand and assisting her to rise.

"A minx I may be," she said, instantly pulling her hand from his, "but I know who Zach Flynn might approach with impunity and who he would be wise to avoid. You do not. Believe me, only I can guide you through the wilds of Bexham."

Vincent said nothing for several moments, much struck by the information that Flynn's dalliances might further jeopardize his chances of finding evidence. He had been prepared to face angry parents whose sons had taken part in the attempted robbery, but he had not reckoned on confrontations with cuckold husbands.

Miss Morgan was correct, he was walking into unfamiliar territory; moreover, territory that was more hostile than he had anticipated. But had he the right to use her as his guide? To include her in what could be a dangerous undertaking? What if someone wielding a firearm should try to dissuade him from his investigation, and she became caught in the cross fire?

He needed time to think.

"Will you walk with me?" he asked, capturing her hand once again and placing it in the crook of his arm. "There is a footpath of sorts just beyond the beech trees."

He did not wait for her answer, but it was just as well, for Janine was not certain she could have spoken. At the mere touch of Vincent's fingers, her heart had doubled its normal number of beats. Then, not content with galloping at a dangerous speed, the foolish organ had practically jumped into her throat once he placed her hand upon his arm.

Vincent must have taken her silence for assent, for he began leading her toward the thicket.

As they approached the overgrown path that led down a gradual incline to what had once been a charming little pond and folly, Janine kept her eyes focused upon her feet, as though she feared she might slip upon the coarse grass. Actually, her intense concentration had nothing to do with the deplorable condition of the path, and everything to do with the shameless amount of enjoyment she was deriving from feeling Vincent's hard, masculine forearm beneath the thin lawn of his shirtsleeve.

Pleasurable sensations reverberated from her palm all the way to her toes, and Janine would have been content to prolong the experience indefinitely, if only Cousin Hortense had not intruded upon her conscience.

"Disgraceful baggage!" the old harridan accused. *"Have you no pride? Must you cling to the man like some pathetic ape leader?"*

Hearing her cousin's voice, almost as if the mean-spirited woman were actually following behind her on the path, Janine withdrew her hand.

Though it was easy enough to break contact with Vincent, it was not so easy to ignore the sense of loss she felt, or the cold loneliness that assailed her once she was separated from his warmth. Unprepared for such an unnerving reaction, and unwilling for him to see just how much touching him had affected her, she turned her face away, cursing herself for allowing her deceased cousin's bitter philosophy to mandate her behavior once again.

Be warned, you old she-dragon! If I should chance to meet Vincent in my next life, I mean to be the world's most brazen hussy!

"A wise move," Vincent said, startling her into wondering if she had spoken her thoughts. "The path is much too narrow for us to walk side by side. Let me go first, then you may put your hand upon my shoulder. I promise not to let you fall."

Not let me fall?

The words echoed in Janine's brain, and with a sudden foreboding that threatened to make her knees buckle, she questioned the possibility of Vincent's promise having come a trifle late.

Of course, he had meant that he would protect her from taking a tumble down the path, but from the way her heart had reacted to the feel of his arm beneath her palm, Janine began to wonder if she needed protection from another type of fall altogether. A far more serious tumble—into love.

Warning herself not to let that happen, to guard against touching him in the future, or even thinking about touching him, she put her mind to the more critical problem of getting him to agree that they should work together.

"There used to be a little stone bench at the water's edge," she said. "If it still stands, we could pause there until you decide what you wish to do."

Since he did not remind her that he had already informed her of his decision, Janine drew hope from his silence—hope that he was considering her arguments.

The bench was still in place, though it listed forward somewhat and was decidedly green with moss, and just beyond it stood an old black poplar Janine remembered from her childhood. Perhaps sixty feet tall, and dwarfing a pair of whitebeam trees, whose pale leaves shimmered in the gentle breeze, the poplar had always offered summer shade to those who would linger for a time beside its massive trunk.

Though she required no shielding from the late afternoon sun that was painting the sky a vivid red and orange, Janine breathed a sigh of contentment. It was the universal sigh of the pilgrim who has come home after a long journey and found at least one thing still the way it had been remembered.

Looking up into the branches of the stately tree, Janine spied a pair of wood pigeons. One of the birds, shyer than its mate, flew away, a turnip top held firmly in its beak, while the other called after it, *Hoo, hoo, coo, coo, hoo.*

"The pigeon with the turnip showed wisdom," Vincent said quietly. "Perceiving herself to be in danger, she flew away while she could."

Janine knew he was not really talking about birds; just as she knew from his voice that he was beginning to yield to her arguments that they join forces. "But I cannot fly away," she said. "Nor would I even if it were possible."

Seating herself upon the bench, she watched Vincent walk to the edge of the pond and search out a small stone. With a flick of his wrist, he caused the stone to skip three times across the scummy surface of the water. It sank quite near the miniature Greek temple that stood in the center of the pond, an algae-covered monument to the folly of a previous generation.

He searched for a second stone. "Time is of the essence," he said, as though informing a confederate of an important detail. "I must return to London by Saturday morning. And when I arrive, I must have proof of my innocence. I cannot fail."

"But that is but three days from now. What is so important about returning on Saturday?"

This time the stone skipped five times. "Do you recall that I told you the older Mr. Neville did not believe his grandson's beating was an act of random violence?"

"Yes, I remember. You said he believed you to be the perpetrator of the crime."

"True. In fact, he is so convinced of my guilt that he has called me out. We are to meet at Hampstead Heath, Saturday at dawn."

Janine felt as though an invisible fist had dealt her a blow to the heart. "He has challenged you to a duel?"

"Yes. And unless I can show him that he is mistaken in his accusation, I must honor the challenge."

They were silent for some time, both lost in thought; Vincent staring off beyond the pond at a bank of dark pink ragged robin, and Janine concentrating upon the amber ribbon she had wound around her fingers, the maltreated satin pulled so taut it bode fair to tearing in two.

When Vincent finally spoke, he did not turn around, but continued to look past the little Grecian temple. "God forgive me," he said, "but I have decided to accept your offer of help."

Janine relaxed, letting go the ribbon. "You will not regret it."

"I regret it already." From the sound of his voice, he spoke through clenched teeth. "And if you should sustain an injury—"

"I will not. After all, why would anyone in Bexham wish to harm me?"

"I pray heaven that question does not wind up on your gravestone."

"I assure you I will come to no harm, but if it will make you feel any better about your decision, I am prepared to make you a promise—the same promise you extracted from your cousin. I will do only what you tell me."

He turned then, a skeptical look upon his face. "Truly? You will follow my instructions—all of them—to the letter? Somehow, I find that hard to believe."

Janine raised her right hand, as if taking an oath. "You have my word that I will be obedient. Although," she added, lowering her hand rather quickly, "I must tell you, in all fairness, that obedience goes somewhat against the grain with me."

At this last, Vincent chuckled. "I shall take that as a warning, Miss Morgan, and not push you too far. Believe me, I have not forgotten that violent streak in you."

Not wanting to show him how relieved she was to see him smile again, she said, "For heaven's sake, must you continue to call me Miss Morgan?"

"Not if you should not wish it, ma'am."

"I do not wish it. Nor do I choose to hear 'ma'am' every other sentence. Since we will be working quite closely these next few days, 'tis silly for us to be so formal."

"I could not agree more. If it is informality you desire, informality you shall have." With a light of mischief in his gray eyes, he said, "I shall follow Miss Craven's example and call you 'my love.' "

Chapter 8

Janine was almost at the beech copse before she realized that she had left Vincent back at the pond. She had hurried away without a word, unable to sit there and make small talk while "my love" kept echoing in her brain, rendering her incapable of coherent thought.

Odd how those words, when spoken by Miss Evangeline, were but another form of address, while upon Vincent's lips they became a verbal caress capable of sending little shivers of delight coursing through her body.

"Wait," he called, catching up with her at that spot beside the copse where the path widened. "What is your hurry, my love?"

"Do not call me that!"

"But you said—"

"I know exactly what I said, and not even in my wildest dreams did I give you permission to so address me."

"Ah," he said, bending quite close to her ear and speaking softly, "so you have wild dreams. May one inquire as to—"

"Sir!" Though she knew him to be teasing her, Janine could not still the heat that rushed to her face. "You go beyond the line."

Straightening, he sighed dramatically. "First you

say, 'Forget *Miss Morgan.*' Then you bid me eschew *ma'am*. And now you disapprove of my third choice. I see there is no pleasing you."

"I meant that you should call me by my name."

Looking skyward, he said, "Heaven grant that it does not begin with an M."

Aware of how ridiculous the conversation had become, Janine laughed. "Allow me to inform you, sir, that you are quite shameless to call upon the saints in heaven, when I misdoubt you have much more in common with the denizens of the nether regions."

He placed his hand over his heart, as though he had been dealt a telling blow. "I am found out. But please, my love, do not apprise Miss Craven of my true character, for I am desirous of preserving that lady's good opinion of me."

"Ha! Too late for that, for Miss Evangeline saw through you from the outset. And lest you think your little ploy to distract me succeeded, be advised that it did not. You still may not address me by that . . . that . . ."

He looked at her with eyes as innocent as can be said of a man wearing a knife strapped across his chest. "What may I not call you?"

"You know full well to what I refer. Do not call me your . . . your love."

"But I must, my love, for you still have not told me your name."

Because they had arrived at the open door of the kitchen, she lowered her voice. "You had only to ask. My name is Janine."

"Janine." Vincent repeated the name several times, as though trying it out upon his tongue, then he shook his head. "A pretty name, to be sure, but I find I have grown accustomed to—"

"Abominable creature!" she muttered, "I warn you."

"Warn him of what?" asked Miss Evangeline, from across the kitchen.

The lady sat near the hearth, in a faded blue satin slipper chair that must have been reclaimed from one of the rooms in the main part of the house. Opposite the chair, leaning negligently against the rustic mantel, was Vincent's young cousin. From the animated look upon the older lady's face, it appeared that she and the gentleman were getting along famously.

Janine felt her cheeks grow warm at the thought of explaining to her former teacher just what it was she did not wish to be called. Thankfully, Vincent came to her rescue.

Stepping across the threshold, he made the lady a bow, then took it upon himself to answer her question. "Your former pupil was warning me, ma'am, of the dangers I might encounter should I venture into the village in the guise of Zach Flynn."

"I fear it is quite true, young man." Then, turning to Janine, she said, "Lest you have forgotten one or two hazards, my love, pray enlighten us as to your catalog of perils."

Again, Vincent answered for her. "They were too numerous to mention, ma'am, but topping the list was irate husbands."

Far from being shocked, Miss Evangeline nodded her agreement. "Reprehensible, but true. Quite the rogue is our Zach."

Since no one saw fit to reply to this observation, Vincent's cousin seized the opportunity to ask him if he meant to go in to the village.

"I believe I must. Despite the warnings of both ladies."

"Capital!" said the young man. "For Miss Craven

was just telling me that there is to be a fair outside Bexham tomorrow."

After a dinner which Gareth declared the finest he had eaten since his return to school for the Easter term, the foursome retired to the snug sitting area Miss Craven had caused to be arranged around the fireplace. The two ladies disposed themselves in chairs while Gareth perched upon a three-legged stool quite near Miss Craven. For his part, Vincent contented himself with leaning against the mantel.

"Furthermore," Miss Craven said, continuing a conversation started at table, "I am convinced they allow you too much license up at Cambridge. If you were a pupil of mine, young sir, there would be no more of this foolish behavior. Depend upon it, I should make you toe the mark."

Not offended in the least, Gareth replied, "For you, ma'am, I should be delighted to toe ten marks. But no more than ten, that being the precise number of digits I grew."

Though there was a hint of amusement in her voice, the lady pretended disdain. "Try for a little conduct, Mr. Henley. It was your behavior we were discussing, not your appendages."

"But, ma'am, it was you who brought up the subject of toes. I merely—"

"You are a thoroughly disrespectful young man," she said, "And should I ever have your poor, beleaguered father's ear, I will advise him to waste no time in thrashing you soundly. An occurrence, I have no doubt, which was sorely missing in your upbringing."

Gareth pretended to be quaking with fear, and at this further impertinence, Miss Craven reached over and gave him a sharp rap upon the knuckles with her fan.

Vincent smiled at their obvious enjoyment of one another, despite the disparity in their ages. However, recalling that the lady had experienced a very busy day, he was about to suggest that he and his cousin return to the coach house so the ladies might enjoy a bit of quiet, when Gareth turned to Janine.

"I collect, ma'am, that Miss Craven was a formidable preceptress. Were you a conscientious student?"

Janine shook her head. "I fear not, Mr. Henley. As Miss Evangeline can attest, I never gave my full attention to such pursuits as studying the globe and working sums, for I was quite certain that I should never have need of either of those boring subjects.

"Being a headstrong and foolish girl, I was forever sneaking off to some secluded spot to lose myself in a book of maudlin poetry or a gothic novel from the lending library. As you may suppose, in order to have time for my own pursuits, I hastened through my school assignments in a decidedly slapdash manner. A habit I now repent in leisure."

"You were very young," Miss Craven said gently.

"And very imprudent," Janine added. "Finding suitable employment is difficult enough for a female. If she is poorly educated into the bargain, the difficult becomes nearly impossible."

"But, my love, you could not have known you would one day need to make your own way in the world."

"No, I could not."

Smiling, as though it were a good joke on her, Janine said, "What a pity I did not possess a crystal ball, so that I could look into the future. If I had, you may depend upon it, I would have applied myself most diligently."

"Are you employed at the moment, Miss Morgan?" Gareth asked.

"For three years I was companion to an elderly cousin. However, as a result of my cousin's demise four weeks ago, I am presently at liberty."

Vincent had watched Janine's face as she said she was at liberty, and though her manner was light-hearted enough to deceive a casual observer, he was not fooled. The lack of sparkle in her eyes gave the lie to her smile.

So. That is why you have returned to this dilapidated house, my friend. You have no place else to go, and no promise of future employment.

Vincent could see that she was worried, and from what he knew of the situation, she had every reason to be.

She had obviously come home hoping for assistance from Sir Burton, and far from receiving the support a sister might reasonably expect, she had found her brother gone and her home uninhabitable. And worse yet, she had now to face the possibility that her only living relative was a criminal who might soon be facing arrest for fraud and felonious assault.

Vincent's hands balled into fists. *Devil take her brother for not appreciating her as she deserved. Why did the selfish lout not make it his business to see that she was protected and cared for? How could he just leave her to fend for herself in a world that was so seldom kind?*

Vincent was already troubled by the knowledge that if he took Sir Burton and Zach Flynn back to town to answer for their crimes, Janine would suffer both embarrassment and emotional pain. Now that he knew the whole of her situation, however, he was doubly concerned.

What would become of her once the sordid story became public? Where could she go? Who would offer her assistance? Even if she had been Miss

Craven's star pupil, no respectable family would employ a young woman whose brother was in prison.

And she would not turn to *him* for help; of this Vincent was certain.

Though he possessed a fortune, and could make her his pensioner without even noticing the cost, he knew Janine would not take money from him. Had he not asked her that very morning if she needed funds, and received a decidedly frosty response? Her negative reply had been delivered swiftly, and with her back straight and her head held high. Not that he did not admire her for her pride, but it made it difficult to know what was best to do.

He had learned while still a boy how frightening the world could be for one without family and funds. And if it was tough for a lad, how much more difficult must it be for a young woman? At least *he* had been strong enough to work in the cane fields, and able to defend himself against those who thought to prey upon him.

For a female of gentle birth, there were only a few possible occupations: governess, companion, perhaps secretary to a lady of high rank. Of course, marriage offered the most security against the harshness of life, but Vincent had not been in the jungle so many years that he had forgotten the ways of polite society. For a woman without sufficient dowry, marriage was not always an option. London was filled with women who were obliged to settle for the protection of a temporary arrangement.

At the thought of someone offering Janine a carte blanche, Vincent was suddenly overcome by a desire to push his clenched fist through the unknown blackguard's face. When he raised it to do so, however, he realized that the cad existed only in his imagination. Looking about him, and discovering that none of the threesome had noticed his action, he relaxed his fingers and ran them through his hair, as if that had been his intention all along.

Janine was among friends at the moment, and for that Vincent was thankful. But he knew the situation was purely temporary. She could not remain with Miss Craven indefinitely, for that lady was obliged to make her own way in the world. As for what would become of Janine in the future, that depended upon what became of her brother.

Of only one thing was Vincent certain, that he would not leave her to the mercies of an unforgiving society.

Wanting a quiet place in which to think about how aiding her was to be accomplished, he bid his cousin make his bow to the ladies. Once the amenities were observed, he and Gareth quit the pleasant kitchen to seek the dubious comforts of the servants' quarters in the coach house.

The next day dawned bright and sunny, with just a hint of a breeze. It was weather made to order for a village fair, as well as for the carrying out of Vincent's plans. Last night, as he lay upon the narrow wooden cot, with its lumpy straw mattress and its musty-smelling blanket, he decided that the fair offered him the perfect excuse for venturing into Bexham. Also, with so many people around, he would not appear so conspicuous as he searched for clues to the whereabouts of Zach Flynn.

Now, while he saw to the needs of the growing number of horses in the stable, he reviewed his strategy. If Flynn could successfully pass himself off as Vincent Thornton, the seventh Baron Thornton, surely *he* could accomplish the reverse. He would pretend to be Flynn, at least for as long as he could do so without coming face to face with someone disposed to put a bullet through his chest, and while in that guise he would keep his ears open for any chance remark that might lead him to the bogus baron.

Naturally, Vincent would have preferred to go to Bexham alone, without the questionable assistance of Janine and his cousin. And even though he had agreed that they might help him, he was more than tempted to fling a saddle on Amigo's back and ride out before either of his helpers was awake.

Almost as if the thought of Gareth had conjured him up, the lad strolled into the stable. His blond hair was mussed, and a wide yawn distorted his handsome face. "Good morning, Cousin," he said, his youthful voice still thick with sleep. "Is it not a perfect day for the fair?"

Janine was prepared to admit that Gareth handled Scheherazade's ribbons with competence, keeping both horse and trap moving along at a steady pace. She was even willing to concede that their moving at all was no small accomplishment, considering the number of people who clogged the road. They had already passed two farmers pushing carts filled with produce, a laborer who carried a pair of geese—both alternately hissing and honking at any traveler who chanced to pass too close—and a dozen or so people who traveled on foot. However, driving with the young man in the trap was not the way she had hoped to travel to the fair.

If anyone had bothered to ask her opinion on the subject, Janine would have told them she preferred riding with Vincent, on Amigo, as she had done yesterday. Not that Miss Evangeline would have approved. Far from it. That lady would have deemed it totally inappropriate for a respectable female to ride double with a man, her arms around his slim waist.

Appropriate or not, Janine still wished she were with Vincent. She watched wistfully as he encouraged the gelding around a family consisting of a laborer in a smock, corduroy breeches, and cap, his flaxen-haired wife in her faded blue calico, and no less than nine young children, all chattering excitedly at the prospect of a day's entertainment.

Following Vincent's lead, Gareth flicked the whip above the roan's head, prompting her to pick up the pace. Once the family was behind them, he remarked upon the mare's responsiveness. "A pretty behaved animal," he said.

"Scheherazade is a love. Believe me, sir, Miss Evangeline paid you quite a compliment to entrust her to your care."

The young man uttered a sound very like a hoot. "I can hardly credit that to be so, ma'am; especially when I consider the last thing the lady said to me before we left the stable yard."

"And what was that, pray?"

"Miss Craven advised me that should the roan so much as throw a shoe, she would personally ensure that my remains were shipped back to Hereford in a bandbox—a *small* bandbox."

Janine could not hide her smile at her friend's threat. "She likes you, sir."

"I will accept your word upon the subject, ma'am, but if that is friendship, I shall try never to get on the lady's list of enemies."

Knowing he was teasing, and that he was very nearly as excited about the fair as the children they had just passed, Janine did not contradict him, but let him continue in a similar manner for the next mile or so. She was obliged to add little to the conversation, speaking only when he commented upon the peculiarity of several dozens poles seen in a distant clearing.

"They are for hop vines," she informed him. "Or, at least, they were once used for that purpose. Obviously those particular poles have been abandoned."

"Seems a pity," Gareth said, "To abandon such a good cash crop. Especially in these hard times, when corn prices are so disastrously low. I should think a farmer must always find a good market for hops. After all, 'tis hops that put the zest in our ale."

"Perhaps. But the vines require a complicated system of poling which, in their turn, require a great expenditure of labor. And even after the soil is dug and the vines are trained upon the poles, there is no guarantee of crop success."

To the gentleman's questioning look she replied, "Bugs and fungus."

"Ah, yes. Bugs. They plague the crops of Hereford as well."

"Pray, sir, tell me of Hereford, for I have never been there. Is it very beautiful?"

"The prettiest country in the whole of England," he replied.

He followed up this bit of undisguised partiality by taking full charge of the conversation for the next twenty minutes, amusing Janine with stories of his home and his childhood, and leaving her free to give the lion's share of her attention to the tall, broad-shouldered man who rode just ahead of them.

Dressed once again in the bottle-green coat, Vincent had also donned a cravat—borrowed from his cousin, no doubt—and a pair of fawn breeches Janine had not seen previously. Thus attired, he was unbelievably handsome, and Janine found it amazing that a man who thought nothing of performing menial tasks that rendered him quite thoroughly filthy, should be at all other times fastidiously clean. Except for the ever-thickening facial hair, Vincent was as neat as any gentleman on the strut in London or Bath.

And his seat upon a horse was superior to almost any gentleman's. Watching him, Janine could not help but notice that he and Amigo appeared almost to glide over the rough road. Man and horse seemed as one, so well did the gelding respond to the slightest pressure of Vincent's knees, obeying instantly the gentle commands.

Vincent had a way with animals. It was as if they trusted him.

Her father had always held it to be true that one could read a man's character in the way he treated his cattle. Of course, being a young girl at the time, Janine had thought the homily just another example of her parent's antiquated notions. Lately, however, she was beginning to think the theory might possess a certain validity. Especially since she trusted Vincent every bit as blindly as did the horses.

This morning, when he had told her he was going to the fair as Zach Flynn, she had not even tried to dissuade him from his purpose. "Let me get my bonnet," was all she had said. Even though she feared for his safety should he encounter Cal Aylesworth, she had come back out to the stableyard ready to do all within her power to help Vincent in his impersonation, trusting him to tell her the truth of what he discovered, even if it proved that Zach was not the man he sought.

The steady *clop, clop* of the mare's hoofbeats, combined with Gareth's unceasing commentary, whiled away the remaining minutes of the trip, and very soon they rounded a bend that put them within sight of the old stone bridge and the little brook it crossed.

Just before they reached the bridge, Vincent lifted his hand, signaling his intention of leaving the road. His destination was a shady spot near the bank of the brook, where an enterprising fellow in an ill-fitting brown coat and a battered straw hat had strung a rope between two giant oak trees. One saddled horse was already tied there.

"Tuppence," the man called out. "Tuppence to mind your 'orse while you enjoy the fair." Waving Vincent forward, he continued to hawk his services. " 'Tis a fine animal, sir, but you've no need to worrit on 'is account. 'E'll come to no 'arm 'ere, and I got me a lad wot'll fetch a pail of water to give 'im a swig or two as the day grows long."

When Gareth followed Vincent, the man began to wave him over as well. "Plenty of room for the trap," he called. "You'll not be wanting to drive farther, sir, for the road be jammed with folk as 'ave come for the day. Best leave your 'orse 'ere where 'e'll be took good care of, and all for the modest sum of tuppence."

After dismounting and giving Amigo into the man's keeping, Vincent tossed him a coin.

"Gor blimey!" the man said, his mouth dropping open at the glitter of gold. "A yellow boy!"

"There will be another guinea for you when I return," Vincent said, "but only if these two horses have received your personal attention."

The man slipped the coin inside his coat, then removed his hat, bowing as though to a king. "Yes, sir. Just as you say, sir. Me own son won't get better care than these 'orses."

Quite as stunned as the man by the sight of the gold coin, Janine said not a word, though her thoughts were running at breakneck speed. *How could Vincent afford to toss guineas around as though they were pebbles in a pond?*

She had assumed he was as destitute as she was. Otherwise, why would he not have put up at the inn, where he could be comfortable? Had he money, then? Obviously his cousin thought so, for Gareth paid not the least attention to the coin, almost as if such an expenditure was a common occurrence.

As Vincent strolled toward her, she asked herself, not for the first time, who he was. And this time, she wanted very much to know the answer.

It had not seemed terribly important before, not when there had been so much other information to assimilate, but suddenly his identity took on real significance. She knew almost nothing about him—not even his full name. He had told her that he had spent a number of years in South America, and she knew that he was searching for the man who had impersonated him and left him to bear the blame for a crime he did not commit. But that was all she knew of him.

While trying to recall anything he had said that she might have overlooked, a rather startling idea suddenly occurred to Janine: Would charlatans go around impersonating beggars?

Of course they would not! Where was the profit in that? If an imposter went to the trouble of usurping another person's identity, it would stand to reason that the person must be a man of wealth or influence.

Was Vincent—could he possibly be—a man of wealth?

While Janine pondered this disturbing new question, the source of her unsettling thoughts approached the trap and held his arms up to help her alight.

"Allow me," he said, catching her by the waist and lifting her down before she had time to say him yea or nay. Once her feet were on the ground, he did not step away from her, as she expected, but captured her hand and placed it firmly within the crook of his right arm, as though he had every right to do so, holding it close against his side. Then, without so much as a by your leave, he began walking toward the bridge.

With great forbearance, Janine chose not to admonish him for this easy familiarity, though honesty compelled her to admit, if only to herself, that it was not tolerance that stayed her tongue; it was breathlessness. Her head might be filled with all manner of questions about his identity and his circumstances, but that did not stop her foolish heart from beating wildly at his nearness.

As they strolled together, she stole a glance at the rugged profile of this man—this stranger. Aside from the fact that he had only to touch her to make her lungs forget their purpose as a life-sustaining organ, what did she know of him?

Looking her fill of his handsome face, she told herself the examination was purely for the purpose of gaining knowledge. After all, a seeker of truth need not apologize for enjoying the subject. After taking note of the way the stark white of his cravat accentuated his deeply tanned skin, she observed as well the way the corners of his eyes were permanently crinkled, as though he had spent years squinting into the sun. These two facts seemed to support his story of having lived in South America. But what of the other years of his life? Where had they been spent?

Vincent turned suddenly, catching her scrutinizing his face, but far from taking it for the rude act it was, he smiled down at her in a way that put all else from her mind—all save his gray eyes.

"Did I tell you," he said quietly, the rich timbre of

his voice all but mesmerizing her, "that I like your frock?"

She shook her head, thanking the gods for prompting her to don the sprigged muslin her cousin Hortense had proclaimed much too youthful for a woman of Janine's years.

"It suits you," he said. "It is as refreshing as your smile, and as unpretentious as your manners."

Gratified by such unexpected gallantry, Janine felt the corners of her mouth begin to turn upward in a smile. But having just heard her manners referred to as unpretentious, she was suddenly embarrassed lest Vincent think her purpose in smiling was to elicit further compliments. Not knowing what was best to do, she schooled her lips to remain as they were, then turned her attention to the sleeve of the Pomona green spencer she wore over the sprigged muslin.

Concentrate, Janine. Focus upon the scalloped braid adorning the cuff. Fix your attention upon the way it matches the cambric of the spencer. Do whatever is needed to keep yourself from looking at him.

As she studied her sleeve where her arm rested upon Vincent's, she noticed a minuscule amount of skin showing between her glove top and the braided cuff of the spencer. Vincent must have noticed it, too, for to her surprise, he placed his left hand over hers, and slowly ran the tip of his thumb beneath the cuff.

As he traced his thumb back and forth across the exposed flesh at her wrist, shivers of delight flowed up her arm. The bridge, the brook, the unanswered questions, all seemed to disappear; Janine was aware of nothing but Vincent and this simple, yet astonishing caress.

"Nice braid," he said softly, leaning so close she could smell the clean, spicy scent of his soap. "And such a pretty color."

Not if her life depended upon it could she have acknowledged his compliment, for she had been robbed of speech by the magic of his touch.

"That shade of green lends a warm, golden glow to your ivory skin."

She looked up at him then, and he rewarded her with a slow smile that seriously impeded her breathing.

"And I suppose I need not tell you," he continued, "what it does to your eyes."

"My . . . my eyes?" she asked in a bemused manner, more than willing to listen to his opinion upon the subject.

"You must know that the pupils are—"

"What's this about pupils?" Gareth asked, catching up with them at the bridge. "Are we to discuss schools on such a splendid day as this? An unforgivably insipid topic, Cousin, I assure you, and one I long to forget. Especially," he added, not even noticing that Vincent's hand had been covering Janine's, or that he had removed it unobtrusively, "when I have every intention of enjoying the fair to the fullest."

"I thought you might have that intention," Vincent said.

The sarcasm was not lost on his young cousin, though the gentleman took it in good part. "Never fear, I am not one of those slowtops who can do only one thing at a time. While I visit the various attractions, I shall be ever alert, keeping my eyes and ears open for any news that would be of interest to you."

Chapter 9

Not by so much as a raised eyebrow did Vincent reveal his possible opinion of persons who tried to juggle two dissimilar activities at once. "Perhaps you might start at the north end," he suggested, "near that tent with the blue and yellow pennant. In the meanwhile, Miss Morgan and I will start at the south end."

"An excellent scheme, Cousin. That way we shall cover twice the ground."

"True. And should we meet some place in the middle, kindly refrain from acknowledging our relationship. Of all the things I have heard of Zach Flynn, none included the existence of a cousin."

After conceding the wisdom of anonymity, Gareth took himself off. Hurrying across the old stone bridge, he fell in with an excited group of locals who were bound for the half-dozen acres of fairgrounds. Having spied their destination just ahead, the group quickened their pace, their noise level swelling with each step.

In the distance were bunting-draped stalls loaded with local produce and crafts, and beyond the stalls, multicolored tents whose high-flying banners proclaimed their exhibits of horses, dogs, and all manner of farm animals.

For the less serious-minded, there were games of chance—booths where one might, for a penny, try one's skill at tossing a ball or a ring at some object, in hopes of taking home a prize. And lastly, there were the various shows with their drummers, their flute players, and their barkers hawking the performances.

Once each year, these few acres of serene country-side were transformed into a place of excitement, and from the speed with which the noisy crowd moved, no one wished to miss a single minute of the gaiety.

Vincent and Janine moved at a more decorous pace, ignoring the blare of the trumpets announcing the official opening of the fair. As they passed quite close to the deserted alehouse, Janine thought she saw some-one attempting to peer through one of the grime-encrusted windows on the second floor. Beholding the face, which was distorted by the filthy glass, she could not suppress a gasp.

"What is it?" Vincent asked.

"I saw someone in the alehouse. Up there. At that window."

Vincent looked where she indicated. "I see no one."

"He was there, nonetheless."

After a few moments further perusal of the boarded-up door and the crumbling facade, he returned his attention to her. Then, as if hoping to tease her back into a lighter mood, he lowered his voice, employing a deep, sepulchral tone. "Perhaps the place is haunted."

Janine shook her head, not so much as a denial of ghostly inhabitants as to dislodge the memory of the face that while contorted, had appeared somehow familiar. "It certainly looks disreputable enough to sport a headless specter or two."

Abandoning his teasing, Vincent said, "Forgive me for having introduced such a fanciful notion. I should not have done so. The old alehouse may have witnessed many spirits, but I daresay they were all the kind poured from a bottle."

Calling herself a fool for giving the incident a moment's thought, Janine turned her back on the ramshackle structure. "It is of little matter. Let us put it from our minds and do that for which we have come here—let us see what may be discovered of Zach Flynn and my brother."

Suiting the action to the word, they followed the crowd to the fair. Unfortunately, after more than an hour had passed, Janine and Vincent had discovered nothing.

They had wasted several minutes exchanging pleasantries with a farmer's apple-cheeked wife, who sat atop a tall, three-legged stool, overseeing the selling of her homemade cheeses, only to discover that she had been born in a neighboring village and had never met Sir Burton. At another booth, an old man with painfully gnarled hands, and a display of exquisitely carved pipes and snuff boxes, had confused Sir Burton with Janine's father, informing her in no uncertain terms that the gentleman was dead these four years and more.

At the remaining booths they received nothing but suspicious stares and stone silence from the people they questioned, and when they approached a horse seller who seemed talkative enough, he was too concerned with haggling over prices with prospective buyers to care who was looking for whom.

In a final attempt to gain what information they might, Vincent had even bantered words with a flirtatious young woman sporting improbable red hair and the gaudy costume of a rope dancer. As Janine had foretold, he wasted his time there, for like the man on stilts, the strolling juggler, and the lad with the performing dog—all of whom mingled among the crowd to entice them to visit the shows—the woman was one of the performers who traveled with the fair, and therefore unacquainted with any of the locals.

Apparently, no one possessed any knowledge of Sir Burton's whereabouts. And since Vincent had successfully passed himself off as Zach, he was prohibited from bringing up that name. The only bright spot in their morning was the fact that they had not encountered Cal Aylesworth.

"What now?" Janine asked.

Vincent shook his head. "I confess to being at an impasse. Could it be that my face is hindering our search?"

"I do not believe so. From what I have observed, your impersonation of Zach Flynn seems to fall into that category known as pearls cast before swine. So far, no one seems even remotely interested in the fellow's comings and goings."

"A surprise, is it not, considering what you and Miss Craven led me to believe."

He looked pointedly to left and right. "Not a jealous husband in sight."

"More than likely," she replied, not meeting his eyes, "they are keeping their distance because you are with me."

"More than likely," he said, the sarcasm not lost on his companion.

To give the conversation a different turn, Janine closed her eyes, breathing deeply and dramatically. "Umm," she said, "I smell something delicious." When he said nothing, she sniffed the air meaningfully. "And unless I am sadly mistaken, the aroma is that of brambleberry tarts." Turning her face up to his, she batted her eyelashes and sighed. "Do you not just adore brambleberry tarts?"

"No," he said, trying not to smile. "I do not. And

allow me to inform you, minx, that I am not one of those fellows you females believe you can wheedle out of his last groat simply by gazing at him in that little-girl-lost manner."

While delivering himself of this diatribe, Vincent reached inside his pocket and pulled out a coin. "Here," he said, hailing the pieman, "the lady will taste your wares."

While Janine munched upon the crusty tart with its gooey, purple filling, they continued their walk, threading their way through knots of people and past booths, exhibits, and games of chance, and as if by common consent they turned in the direction of the one spot at the fair that was not teeming with humanity. It was a large, gold-and-yellow striped tent whose flap had been pinned back, revealing an interior both dim and decidedly musty smelling.

A black-lettered placard, its corners adorned with drawings of oriental carpets and samovars, was affixed to a lacquered finger sign that pointed toward the entrance, the words inviting *Gentlemen Only* to view *Ten Bewitching Beauties Stolen from the Harem of Sheik Abdul of Araby.* Since the promised beauties were to be seen on stage twice daily, at six o'clock and eight o'clock, the tent was unoccupied at the moment.

Across the way from where they stood was a second tent, this one quite small, and upon its fading placard was painted a rather voluptuous Gypsy Fortune-Teller dressed in a bright red skirt and dozens of filmy veils. Jewels adorned her turban, and in her hand she held a crystal ball. Written beneath the picture of the lady was the name, *Madame Tibaldi.*

"When you finish your tart," Vincent said, pointing to the fortune-teller's tent, "I think we should go over there."

Janine looked at the placard, then back at him. "You cannot be serious! Do you expect some fake seer to tell us where we might find my brother?"

He shook his head. "I was not thinking of Sir Burton. However, I am perfectly serious about consulting the—er—Madame."

"You may do as you wish, of course, but I can think of nothing that would induce me to seek the advice of such a person."

"Can you not?" he asked. "Upon seeing the sign, I was reminded of last evening, when you were lamenting your failure to apply yourself to your schoolwork. At that time, you said you wished you had possessed a crystal ball, so that you could have looked into the future."

"But . . ." The remark had been a careless one, the kind of thing one said in jest, and Janine could not believe that Vincent had attached any importance to it.

"I may have said something of the sort, sir, but the future I wished to know about has now become the present, and I promise you, I know the present all too well."

"But you cannot know the *future* future. Here is your golden opportunity to see what lies in store for the coming years."

"Sir, you are being ridiculous."

"Not at all. Come. Be adventurous."

"I cannot," she said. Grasping at the first excuse that entered her head, she showed him her fingers. "Look at me, I am sticky from the tart."

"Easily mended," he said, reaching inside his coat and removing a handkerchief fashioned of fine lawn. Thinking he meant to lend her the snowy white square, Janine reached out for it, but he surprised her by catching her hand and lifting it to his mouth. To her further dismay, he took the tip of her forefinger between his lips and slowly licked away the sugary traces of brambleberry.

Heat burned her face as he applied himself to the pad of her finger, then performed a similar act upon her thumb. The task completed, he wiped both digits upon the handkerchief.

Still reeling from such an intimate act, Janine did not protest when he put his hand beneath her elbow and led her across to the small tent. Nor did she voice any objection when he pulled back the flap and ushered her into the shadowy interior.

Janine required several moments to become accustomed to the dimness, but once her eyes adjusted, she spied an ancient crone sitting at a small, baize-covered table. The woman was dressed in rusted black bombazine, her grayed head covered by a loosely draped scarf, and the only similarity between her and the voluptuous damsel on the placard was the crystal ball that took pride of place on the table.

"Come in," she said, her English heavily accented. "I have been waiting for you."

When the old woman spoke, Janine hesitated. "Vincent, I—"

"Shh," he said, as much to keep her from calling him by his name again as to still her protests. "Stay. See what wonders your future holds. I will be right outside."

Madame Tibaldi stretched out an unbelievably dirty hand and waited for Vincent to place a shilling upon her palm. After examining the coin to be certain of its authenticity, she stashed it in a velvet-lined jewel casket, then gave her attention to the crystal ball, leaning in very close and whispering some sort of incantation over it.

By the time Vincent stepped outside and closed the tent flap, the old woman's words had taken on a quiv-

ering, sing-song quality that put him in mind of the
magic spells favored by some of the witch doctors of
the Amazon tribes.

Janine, not having numbered among her acquaintances even one witch doctor, found the old woman's
murmurings unnerving in the extreme, and she fervently wished that Vincent had not seen fit to leave
her alone with the professed seer.

"Do not worry, my child."

Upon hearing the heavily accented words, Janine
jumped. She had not realized the incantations were at
an end, or that the fortune teller had motioned for her
to be seated in the remaining chair.

"You have nothing to fear from me, my child. I am
an old woman. Frail and lacking in physical strength.
But," she added, tapping a dirty forefinger first at her
temple then at the crystal ball, "these two powers are
with me still."

She lowered her voice to the merest whisper. "I
know what you would ask of me."

"You . . . you do?"

Madame Tibaldi ignored the question, choosing instead to peer into the innocuous-looking glass sphere.
"I see the long road that is your life. It is a winding
road, and one that will require many years to travel
its length."

Surprising herself, Janine breathed a sigh of relief.
"Many years?" she asked hesitantly.

"Very many. Far too many to count. The journey
will be difficult at times, but it will not be undertaken
alone. Another will accompany you. One whose heart
beats in harmony with your own."

When Janine would have asked a question, the old
woman held up her hand impatiently. "Do not plague
me with silly questions of husbands and riches. Such
interrogations are the province of foolish young girls.

You have need of other answers, and I see that which you wish to discover."

She looked up at Janine, her rheumy eyes as piercing as twin daggers. "Are you prepared to listen?"

Wanting to reply in the negative, Janine surprised herself by responding in the affirmative. "I will listen."

"Very good. I shall tell you all you need to know. Please to remain quiet."

With her hands shielding her eyes as if from some bright light, the seer leaned quite close to the crystal ball, whispering to it, and nodding her head as if in acceptance of its answers. After several minutes, she sat up straight and removed the scarf from her head, placing it over the sphere.

"He whom you seek," she said finally, "is close at hand. Be patient, he will find you in due time. But," she added, wagging her finger as if to admonish a naughty child, "he whom you wish to avoid will find you as well. Be vigilant."

The old woman said no more, and in a very few moments her head fell forward, her chin resting upon her chest, as if she slept.

Assuming the session was at an end, Janine rose to leave, feeling quite foolish for having listened to the nonsense, for it was the kind of ambiguous gibberish every member of the trade must recite day after day. She had reached the tent flap and was pulling it aside, when the fortune-teller spoke again.

"Abandon all plans for your next life. Even those made in jest. Concentrate instead upon your present existence. Do only those things which your conscience tells you are right, and this life will be rich with blessings."

After Vincent left Janine with the fortune-teller, he walked over to the larger tent to wait in the shadows.

With nothing else to occupy his time, he searched through the distant crowds for a face that resembled his own. He found no such visage, though he noticed one that was at least familiar. It belonged to the pugnacious wagon driver, one of the ubiquitous McFees.

The young man's clothes were clean and pressed, as if the day was important to him, and upon his bright red hair he sported a new, though cheaply blocked, beaver hat. Pugnacious no longer, his freckled face beamed with pride as he looked at the girl who strolled beside him. His companion, an uncommonly pretty chit, had removed her chip straw bonnet, revealing curling blond hair that was turned the color of golden wheat by the sun's bright rays.

It did not require a needle wit to guess the identity of the fair charmer, especially not after one noted the worshipful way McFee gazed into her green eyes. Unless the village could boast of two such startling beauties, the damsel was none other than Franny Aylesworth, the female generally accepted to be the front runner for Zach Flynn's affections.

Hoping to avoid being seen by the girl, Vincent was about to step behind the placard when, to his regret, he was spotted by McFee. At sight of him, the younger man stiffened, causing his companion to turn and look as well. With a briefly muttered curse at himself for his carelessness, Vincent ducked inside the dim interior of the tent. Unfortunately, he was not fast enough, for within a matter of seconds he heard a soft voice calling Zach's name.

"Are you in there?" she asked. "Zach, darling, it's me, Franny."

If Vincent had not promised Janine that he would be right outside when she finished with the fortune-teller, he would have tried to find some means of escape. Since he could not do so, he moved as far away from the tent flap as possible, to make what use he could of the lack of light. Pulling the brim of his hat down low on his forehead, he awaited the inevitable.

His pursuer stepped further inside the tent. "Zach?" she called again, "where are you?"

"Here," he said, keeping his voice low.

The beauty turned to the sound of his voice, peering at him in the shadows. "Is that you, Zach darling?"

"Hello, Franny."

Chapter 10

Upon hearing her name, the young woman ran toward Vincent, a smile of joy upon her face. "Where have you been?" she asked, throwing herself against his chest and winding her arms around his waist. "I have been so worried."

Not knowing what else to do, Vincent put his arms around her, holding her close, his only design to keep her from looking into his gray eyes. If the orbs had given him away to Miss Craven, surely this girl who loved Zach Flynn would not be deceived.

"You were gone so long," she said. "Were you successful? Did you get the money?"

"Some," he answered noncommittally.

She grew stiff in his arms. "Only some of it?"

"Um hmm," he muttered, still keeping his voice hushed.

"Not all?"

When he said no more, she pulled away from him and turned her back, concealing her face in her cupped hands.

Suspecting that she might be crying, Vincent chose the better part of valor, and remained quiet. After a minute or two, when she spoke again, her voice was choked with tears. "If you didn't win enough to purchase passage for two, did . . . is there enough for *one*?"

Before he could decide what was best to answer,

she threw herself at him again, this time twining her arms around his neck and sobbing as though her heart would break. "Don't sail to America without me," she said between sobs. "Promise me you won't. Please, Zach, I beg you, don't leave me behind. If you go alone, I know I'll never see you again."

Vincent let her cry, patting her shoulder from time to time, not knowing what else to do. Never in his life had he been so desirous of being someplace else. Here he was, wrapped in the arms of a female whose face and form were sheer perfection, and all he could think of was how he might get away from her.

In time, her sobs abated, and when she began to sniff, Vincent reached inside his coat and found his handkerchief. "Here," he said, "dry your eyes, there's a good girl."

Relaxing her hold on him, she took the fine, white lawn and began to wipe away the tears. "You won't leave me, will you, Zach? Swear to me upon your mother's memory that you'll wait until we have all the money. You know I couldn't live without you, for you are my world, my reason to . . ."

Her words seemed to hang, unfinished, in the still, musty air, as she studied the handkerchief she had just refolded in search of a dry corner.

Only just realizing his stupidity, Vincent watched as she traced her finger very slowly over the intricately embroidered initials. His initials. For Vincent Thornton.

After a silence that seemed to last for hours, the girl looked up at him, her green eyes searching for something. "Why haven't you shaved?" she asked, as she reached up and slowly pushed his hat back from his forehead.

Vincent closed his telltale eyes, hoping she would believe he had done so to enhance his enjoyment of her touch. Before he realized what she was doing, she had wound her arms around his neck and was pulling his head down toward hers.

"Kiss me," she said.

Even before he felt her cool, emotionless lips press against his, he knew the charade was over.

The kiss lasted mere seconds before the girl moved away from him. "Who are you?" she asked. "And what have you done with my Zach?"

To Vincent's everlasting gratitude, Janine chose that moment to enter the tent. "Vincent?" she called, her voice just above a whisper, "we must go. Now! Cal Aylesworth is headed this way."

The words had only just left her mouth when Janine realized that the two people in the shadowy interior had been kissing. "I beg your pardon," she stammered. "I did not mean to intrude. Forgive me for—"

"I know you," the woman said, her words almost an accusation. "You are Sir Burton's sister." Hurrying forward, she stopped in front of Janine and caught her by the shoulders. "Where is your brother? Is he still with Zach?"

Janine pulled free of Franny's grasp, but before she could disabuse the girl of her belief that she knew anything of Sir Burton's whereabouts, she heard a loud bellow from outside, not far from the tent.

"Flynn!" yelled an angry male voice. "Show yourself, you bastard!"

The two women looked at each other, their eyes wide with concern, both aware of the violent nature of the owner of the voice, though fearful for the welfare of two different men.

"Flynn, you coward!" Cal yelled again. "You coming out of your hidey-hole, or you want I should come in and drag you out?"

From the murmur of excited voices in the distance, Janine assumed the bully had brought an audience with him to watch the intended beating.

"Drag 'im out," someone yelled. "Then plant 'im a facer for me!"

"That's right, Cal," yelled another, "give 'im what for! Only save me a piece of 'im. On account of I got a score of me own to settle."

"Make his claret run!" a third said.

Several hoots and calls greeted this last suggestion, prompting Janine to brush past Franny and run to Vincent. It was as she suspected, he showed not the least sign of concern.

"There must be a back way out of here," she said. "Surely the harem beauties must avail themselves of some sort of exit when their performances are finished. Help me find it."

When Vincent did not move, Janine caught him by the arm and gave a firm tug. She might as well have attempted to move an oak tree. "Please," she said. "We must go."

"I told you before," he said calmly, "I am well able to defend myself against bullies."

To Janine's surprise, and immense relief, Franny came over to lend her support to the suggestion of flight. "You don't know my brother," she said. "He uses whatever measures are necessary to ensure that he does not lose. Fair fight or foul, it's all the same to him."

When Vincent appeared unmoved by her plea, the girl continued, "But even if Cal was an honorable man, and knew the meaning of fair play, why should you take a beating meant for someone else? Believe me, Zach can fight his own battles, and he won't thank you for your interference."

Though Vincent raised one dark eyebrow, as if interested to hear such a report of his impersonator, he did not budge. Just when Janine despaired of getting him back to Morgan House alive, help came from another source.

"Cousin," Gareth Henley called *sotto voce*. "Quick, come this way."

Janine turned hopefully toward the young man who had squirmed beneath the tent, toward the rear. "Thank God you are come."

"Saw you go in the front way, ma'am. But when I noticed that mob approaching, I decided I had much better seek a back entrance. We must make haste, for they will run out of tents to search any moment now."

She looked once again at Vincent. "Please. Do not face Cal."

"If you mean that giant," Gareth said, "it is not just him you would have to face, Cousin. From what I can see, several in the mob want a piece of you—or a piece of Flynn, I should say. And two of the louts are brandishing cudgels. Cannot best them all. Much better to come away now. Live to fight another day, don't you know."

"Bah!" Franny said. "You and Zach have more in common than your looks. Dolts, both of you, with your foolish male pride. You would face my brother and endanger us all."

Far from angering him, as Janine expected, this last comment seemed to turn the tide. "You are right," he said. He held his hand out to her. "Will you come with us?"

She shook her head. "Do not worry about me, for I have years of experience dealing with Cal. Look to your own safety. If you are very quiet when you leave, and they do not hear you, perhaps I can send them in the wrong direction."

"Thank you," Janine said. "And good-bye."

"Not 'good-bye.' For I mean to come to Morgan House later. I must know what has become of Zach."

"Until later, then," Vincent said.

After holding up the side of the tent so Janine could crawl beneath it, Vincent followed her out. For a time they moved cautiously, then once they were some distance away, he and Gareth each took one of Janine's hands, and the three of them ran as fast as possible toward the stone bridge.

When they reached the bank of the brook, where the horses were tied between the two giant oak trees, Vincent lifted Janine into the trap beside Gareth, then tossed the man in the straw hat his promised guinea. "Put 'em along," he told Gareth.

"But Miss Craven said—"

"I shall make any apologies necessary to Miss Craven, but I do not believe Scheherazade will suffer from a bit of exercise."

Janine could not stop herself from asking Vincent where *he* would be.

"Amigo and I will follow behind, to guard your backs."

Though she could not like the idea, she held her tongue. For the moment, it was enough that they were leaving this place, and that Vincent had allowed himself to be dissuaded from confronting Cal Aylesworth.

The trip home was a far different matter from the earlier ride. First, they traveled dangerously fast—the road appearing a veritable blur beneath them—and second, Gareth seemed to have run out of things to say. It was just as well, for Janine was in no humor for polite conversation.

Due to their near encounter with Cal and the mob of men who accompanied him, she was experiencing a degree of residual fear, manifested in icy cold hands, trembling knees, and a heart that pounded painfully against her ribs. And as if that were not enough, the words of the fortune-teller kept echoing inside her head. Her mind was in a turmoil trying to decipher what the seer's message meant.

Not but what it was foolish beyond permission to give credence to the babbling of a dirty old crone who told fortunes at a fair. Only a fool would do so. Surely no woman in her right mind would give it a second thought.

Of course, if that woman had placed her home, her good name, and even her safety into the keeping of a man she had known for scarcely more than two days, it was arguable if she was, in fact, *in* her right mind.

The conjecture being unanswerable, Janine pushed it from her thoughts, at least until such time as they should reach Morgan House. For the nonce, it seemed imperative that she take thought for her life, for Gareth, obviously bewitched by the thrill of speed, had given the roan the signal to proceed even faster. With the road whizzing beneath them, Janine was obliged to concentrate upon clinging to the trap.

As soon as the windblown, but jubilant young man pulled the mare to a stop in the stableyard, his emotionally taxed passenger jumped down from the trap, not waiting for assistance. Knowing she must appear as disheveled as Gareth, and wanting time alone to gather her thoughts, she chose to absent herself before Vincent arrived.

After running across the forlorn kitchen garden to the rear door of the house, she stopped only long enough to exchange the merest civilities with Miss Evangeline and Chloe, both of whom sat beside the fire, plying their needles. Once that necessary formality was completed, Janine hurried to the privacy of her room, where she could think.

* * *

Thinking, Janine soon discovered, was not at all the same thing as putting one's thoughts in order; the former occurred without effort, while the latter proved frustratingly difficult to achieve. Two hours of privacy were not sufficient for her to solve even one of the mysteries surrounding Vincent. Who was he? And why did he feel the need to conceal his identity? She had no answers, of course, and after reviewing everything she knew of him, he was as much an enigma as ever.

She had been similarly unsuccessful in her bid to understand why she had experienced such fear for his safety. When she had quit the fortune-teller's tent, and spied that bully, Cal Aylesworth, heading in their direction—anger emanating from him like a morning fog rising from a moist road—all she could think of was warning Vincent. Fear had gripped her heart, wrenching it from her chest, and leaving it lodged within her throat.

As for the white-hot anger that had surged through her when she entered the tent and saw Franny Aylesworth kissing Vincent, upon that subject Janine refused to devote even one moment's concentration.

She was not jealous! The very idea was as demeaning as it was ludicrous. After all, she had no claim upon Vincent.

Why, when all was said and done, he and Janine were practically strangers. Vincent meant nothing to her. Nor she to him. And if she had allowed *his* face to become superimposed upon that shadowy figure the fortune teller had said would accompany her on life's journey—the person whose heart would beat in harmony with her own—that, too, meant nothing.

Vincent was the only man she had spent any time with in several years, so it was perfectly logical that his face should come to mind when the old crone said Janine would not travel the road of life alone. Likewise, it was imminently logical that the mysterious man of her future should possess a characteristic or two reminiscent of Vincent. The way he smiled, for instance, with the corners of his mouth turning up a second before that teasing light appeared in his eyes. Or the way he listened when she talked, with his gaze upon her face as if to catch every nuance of her conversation.

Of course, when her foolish thoughts took a giant leap from Vincent's gaze to the memory of how just being near him made her entire body hum with awareness, Janine decided her brain was totally lacking in logic.

The only thing she could do to preserve her sanity was to forget what the fortune-teller had said. Put all thoughts of it from her mind. Wipe the slate clean. Expunge all the pictures of that phantom with Vincent's face. From now on, she would concentrate on only one thing, finding proof that neither Vincent nor her brother had injured the young man in London.

Having reaffirmed her priorities, Janine felt renewed; so much so that she removed the crumpled sprigged muslin—refusing to allow herself to recall that Vincent had liked it, or that he had said it was as refreshing as her smile—and replaced it with a dress that had always been her favorite. Fashioned of azure blue jaconet, the simple frock's only claim to *á la modality* was its Marie sleeves, which were full to the wrist, then tied into compartments by ribbons of a lighter blue.

The last time Janine had worn the dress, a young lady in Bath had admired it, commenting upon its suitability to the wearer's figure. Not that *that* had played any part in Janine's having chosen to wear it today!

Putting such a ridiculous suspicion from her mind, she completed her toilette, then went in search of Miss Evangeline. To her surprise, Chloe was the only occupant of the kitchen.

The maid stood on the far side of the table, a tall cook pot and a cutting board before her, a mound of raw carrots and turnips to her left, and a large knife in her hand. "Be you looking for Miss Evangeline?" she asked, seizing a carrot from the mound and scraping it with quick, rather angry motions.

"I am. Is she resting in her room?"

"Humph. Not her. The young gentleman come and took her out for a breath of air."

"Mr. Henley?"

"That be the one," Chloe replied. "And when I told Miss Evangeline that a woman of her age needed to rest of an afternoon, she paid me not the least heed. Said since we come here, she felt forty again. Claims the country air be acting like a tonic on her."

As if to underscore her disapproval of such behavior in her mistress, Chloe slapped the carrot down upon the cutting board, then raised her knife, delivering the first chop with such ferocity that Janine jumped.

"If you was to ask me, Miss, I'd say it bain't the air what's perked Miss Evangeline up. It's the gentlemen. Acting foolish as her sister, she is."

After giving the carrot several more chops, the maid retrieved the pieces and tossed them into the cook pot. "What gets into spinsters, these days? Don't seem to matter how much schooling they got, just let a gentleman come around, smiling at 'em and paying 'em a little attention, and the lot of 'em start acting like ninnyhammers."

Grabbing another carrot, she gave it the same rough treatment as its predecessor. "You take my advice, Miss, and keep your head about you. Don't start acting like the rest of 'em."

Janine felt heat rise to her face. At twenty-four, she supposed she qualified as a spinster. But had she also joined the ranks of the ninnyhammers? She adjusted one of the ribbons on her sleeve, honesty compelling her to admit that she had donned the blue in hopes of seeing admiration in Vincent's eyes.

"And I'll tell you summit else," Chloe said, apparently wishing to empty her budget, now that she had got started, "though I don't expect you'll pay me no more mind than Rose Flynn did thirty years ago. 'Twas a waste of me breath then, and unless modern females have learned some sense—which I take leave to doubt—it'll be a waste now."

Rightly divining herself as being numbered among those modern females whose clear-headedness was in question, Janine schooled her countenance not to smile, declaring herself willing to listen to whatever Chloe had to say.

Unbending somewhat, the maid abandoned the vegetables for the moment and wiped her hands upon her apron. "Most like, you'll call me an old poke-nose, same as Rose did, but I'll wager that what I have to say be summit your lady mother—God rest her soul—would tell you if she was here."

Curious as to why she and Zach Flynn's mother should warrant the same advice, albeit thirty years apart, Janine said, "Rest assured, I shall not call you a poke-nose."

"Well, I'm sure I thank you, Miss."

After looking about her, as if to be certain that no one else had entered the kitchen, she said, "My advice to you is, you be on your guard where that raven-haired gentleman is concerned."

"Raven-haired gentleman?" Janine stared at the maid. "Do you mean Vincent?"

"I mean him as looks like Zach Flynn. He's a Lunnon swell, as any woman with eyes in her head can plainly see, and I hope I don't have to tell you how such men behave."

Chloe had called him a gentleman. How, Janine wondered, could the maid be so positive about Vincent's status, when she could not? The man was not above getting his hands dirty if a job needed doing, and he never puffed up his consequence. Were those the manners of a London swell?

"I know nothing of London swells, Chloe. How do such men behave?"

"Like care-for-nobodies," she replied. "They come to the country, dressed in their fancy clothes and driving expensive cattle, turning all the young girls' heads, and if they spy a likely lass, they pay her all manner of compliments, hoping for a bit of a romp . . . if you get my drift."

Not waiting for Janine's confirmation, Chloe continued. "'Course, the silly chits believe everything the blackguards tell 'em. Don't matter how many wiser heads warn 'em to beware. Naturally, soon as the swells be finished with whatever business brought 'em from Lunnon in the first place, they high-tail it back to Town. Faster than a body can say, 'Bob's your uncle,' they be gone, and the foolish country lass quickly forgot."

Janine's face burned with embarrassment. Vincent was not like that! He would never act dishonorably. She was as certain of that fact as she was that pennywort grew in the cracks of stone walls.

"Most likely," Chloe said, breaking in upon Janine's thoughts, "all them swells got some society lady waiting for 'em back in Lunnon."

Vincent, and some lady of the ton?

Not wanting to hear such speculation, or to consider such a possibility, Janine muttered something about taking a short walk before dinner; then she hurried from the kitchen before the maid could continue her well-meant counseling.

"You mark my words, Miss," Chloe yelled just before the door closed behind Janine, "acorns don't fall far from the tree."

When she left the house, Janine had no particular destination in mind. All she knew for certain was that she must avoid the stable, for she was sure to find Vincent there, and after what Chloe had just told her, she did not think she could look into his face without blushing.

It had needed a minute or two before she understood the maid's reference to trees, and the landing place of the acorns, and a full minute more before she realized what any of it had to do with Rose Flynn. Now, of course, she saw a connection between Zach and Vincent that had not previously entered her mind—a reason why they looked so much alike. It was possible that they had the same father—the London swell Chloe had warned Rose about.

The man had obviously come to Bexham thirty years ago, spied Rose Flynn, and wooed her. Later, when his business—whatever it was—was completed, he had returned to London, leaving Rose with a very telling reminder of their flirtation.

When he left, had the swell returned to his wife—a society lady who was Vincent's mother? Or was Vincent, like Zach, just another of the Lothario's by-blows?

If that was the case, it would explain why Vincent had spent so many years in the jungles of South America, for no father would send his legitimate son to such a place. It stood to reason that a man of wealth would insist that his heir remain in England, to take his rightful place in society.

More confused than ever about the man who seemed to occupy a disproportionate amount of her thoughts, Janine decided she did, indeed, need a walk before dinner. But not a short one. To sort out such disquieting speculation, she required some real exercise; she needed a long walk, one that would test her strength and sweep the cobwebs from her brain. With this objective in mind, she strode purposefully toward the copse of beech trees and the overgrown foot path she and Vincent had taken yesterday.

Years ago, a neatly graveled walk had continued beyond the place where they had stopped. It had, in fact, circled the pond. Once bordered by informal plantings of blue-eyed forget-me-nots and dainty yellow flag, the walk had been furnished at intervals with stone benches for anyone who needed a respite before completing the three-quarter mile trek, or for those who merely wished to pause and admire the folly from a different perspective.

If any semblance of the old walk remained, Janine meant to travel its length. Several times, if need be.

As with so many plans, however, this one was destined to go astray, for when she made her way down the gradual incline of the path, she discovered that another had come before her.

Tall, raven-haired, and incredibly handsome, Vincent stood near the massive trunk of the black poplar, his gaze fixed upon something beyond the algae-covered folly. As before, the late afternoon sun had been busy with its brush, painting both the sky and the reflecting water with varying shades of gold and red.

Janine paused, unsure what she ought to do. Should she pretend she had not seen Vincent and walk on, or should she speak, letting him know that he was no longer alone?

"Come," he said, not even turning around, "I want to show you something."

Chapter 11

Janine did not bother to ask him how he knew she was there, or what he wished to show her, she just walked over to him, stopping quite close to the water's edge.

"Over there," he said, pointing to a tender young shoot that had been cracked off a pollarded willow and fallen into the pond. "Do you see that dragonfly hovering just above the leaves?"

She nodded.

"Now. Look just beneath the surface of the water. Do you see a fish?"

"I see him."

"He is waiting for the dragonfly to come a little closer. Licking his scaly lips, as it were, in anticipation of the tasty morsel."

"Poor dragonfly."

"It is nature's way," Vincent said. "Though seemingly harsh, it is a system that has worked well for millions of years. Now, watch what happens when I have the effrontery to intervene."

Bending down, he picked up two small stones. Then drawing back his arm, he sent the smaller, flatter of the two skipping across the water. The pebble made four hops, its final one coming very near the willow shoot and startling the dragonfly, causing the insect to flap its delicate wings several times before flying away. As well, at the splash of the pebble, the fish made a hasty retreat.

"I see no cause for repining," Janine said. "Your intervention saved the dragonfly's life."

"True. But suppose the fish was near starvation. What if I, by denying him the insect, have hastened his death? I will have played God, when I am totally miscast for the part."

Not at all certain where this esoteric conversation was leading, Janine remained quiet. She had not long to wait for edification.

"Most of my time in South America was spent on the Amazon River. The gentleman who took me with him on the expedition—the man who was my mentor, and as dear to me as a father—was both a botanist and a naturalist. He had traveled the world, seen civilization in its most primitive and its most sophisticated forms, and from his observation, he had concluded that man's intervention with nature might one day render the entire Earth uninhabitable."

As if in anger, Vincent reached the hand that held the second pebble back toward his shoulder, then putting his weight into the release, threw the stone as hard as he could, hitting the miniature Greek temple. The stone ricocheted off the folly and fell into the water, making dozens of ripples that fanned out toward the shore.

"In coming to Bexham," he said, "I have intervened in several peoples' lives. And like those ripples you see radiating on the water, apparently unending, so might be the effects of my intervention. I begin to wonder if by trying to right one wrong, I have precipitated others."

"Whose lives do you mean?"

"I was thinking particularly of Franny Aylesworth."

"Ah, yes. Franny."

To her chagrin, Janine experienced a momentary wish to have at her disposal the fortune-teller's crystal ball, so that she might look into the future and see the beautiful Franny old and toothless, her honey-blond hair grizzled with age. "I told you she was beautiful."

"Quite lovely," he said. "But I suspect her home life has not been pretty. With such a brother, how can it be anything but difficult? I only hope that by shielding us today, she did not bring Cal's wrath down upon herself."

Janine had the grace to blush for her earlier jealousy. "I had not thought of that."

"I should be surprised if you had. One has a tendency to put bullies from one's mind. Unless, of course, one is obliged to live with them. In that instance, they are never far from one's thoughts and experience." He remained quiet for several moments, almost as if his words had recalled such a person to his mind.

"Also," he continued, after a time, "the girl has hopes of escaping this place. The wounded dove dreams of flying away, of going to America with Zach Flynn for a new start. If I take him back to London, I put paid to those plans."

Janine would not allow this to be Vincent's fault. "But if Zach committed the crime, the fault is his."

"But it is Franny who will pay the price."

Vincent turned then and looked at her, his eyes filled with regret. "And what of you? If I take your brother back, and he is found guilty, what of your chances for the future?"

Unprepared for the question, and unwilling to admit that she had no answer, Janine tried for a light tone. "Who knows what the future may hold? But, I beg you, sir, do not worry on my account. Franny

Aylesworth may be a wounded dove, but I assure you, I am not."

"No," he said, "you and I are like house pets who have been displaced. Just a pair of cats thrust from the home we knew into a cold, harsh world—a world for which we were ill-prepared."

To her surprise, he reached out and gently touched her jaw with the back of his hand, as if she were, indeed, a kitten, smoothing a trail of warmth from her ear to her chin and back again. As his work-roughened skin moved caressingly against hers, her flesh tingled as though alive for the first time, and all coherent thought became impossible.

She looked up into his unreadable eyes. "We . . . we are alike?"

"In a manner of speaking, we are. Although we differ in one very important way."

"I am a girl cat?" she asked.

He smiled. "Make that *two* very important ways in which we differ. For this discussion, however, the most significant difference is that I have grown feral, while you are still tame, with a good chance of finding a new home some day. At least you may do so if I do not spoil it for you."

At that moment, with his powerful hand touching her, stroking her jaw with such tenderness, Janine would have gladly forsaken all her hopes for the future; if only Vincent would come closer. If only he would bend down just a little and kiss her.

"You kissed Franny," she whispered, not even aware of the sudden change of topic.

"No," he said. "Franny kissed me. It was a test to see if I was Zach."

"She could discern that from a kiss?"

"She could and she did."

This talk of kisses was having an odd effect upon

Janine's lips, making them quiver as if in anticipation, like the pulsating of the dragonfly's wings just before he took flight. "Are not kisses all the same?"

"No. Not at all. And I should think they would be decidedly different if a man—or woman—were kissing the person they loved."

To still the strange pulsating, and the growing warmth, Janine ran the tip of her tongue along her bottom lip. Oddly, it had the opposite effect from what she had intended. Far from cooling her mouth, the touch of her tongue seemed to add to the heat. So, too, did Vincent's quick intake of breath.

Why does he not come closer?

As if urged by something inside her she did not understand, Janine leaned toward him. To her delight, the hand that had been caressing her jaw slid around to the side of her neck, the strong, supple fingers curving around her nape, sending tendrils of enchantment down her spine. Meanwhile, Vincent's thumb slipped beneath her chin, gently guiding it upward.

"Have you ever been kissed?" he asked, his voice husky.

"No," she answered, her own voice sounding strangely whispery. "But I should like to be."

Bringing his other hand to her face, Vincent slipped his fingertips beneath the thick sweep of hair that covered her ears, exposing the flesh. Slowly he leaned forward and pressed his firm lips where the hair had been, teasing her skin with slow, tantalizing little kisses that progressed ever closer to the corner of her mouth.

When Janine thought she must surely die from the blend of pleasure and anticipation, he brushed his lips against hers. The contact was so soft, so fleeting, she might have doubted it had happened if she had not experienced that wild surge of joy that seemed to turn her very bones to liquid, making her knees threaten to give way beneath her.

Vincent must have understood her plight, for he released her neck and slid his arm across her shoulder and down her back until he found her waist, pulling her against him and supporting her weight. Happy to be in his arms at last, she stood on tiptoes, so that her face was closer to his, inviting him to do with her mouth what he would.

"Janine," he whispered, gazing into her eyes, his own gray orbs grown dark as the sea on a cloudy day, "you are unbelievably sweet, and I—"

"I collect it was Sir Douglas Morgan, Janine's grandfather, who caused the folly to be constructed."

Miss Evangeline's voice seemed to come from a long way off, so distorted did it sound to Janine, but when Vincent stepped away from her, holding her shoulders lest she fall from the sudden loss of his support, she realized the lady was but a few feet away.

"Actually," her friend continued, "'tis a silly affectation, a Greek temple in an English pond. But there is no explaining the foolish behavior of one's forebears. A pleasant walk, though, do you not agree, Mr. Henley?"

"Oh, very pleasant," Gareth replied, sarcasm in his tone. "Especially with you being so obliging as to supply me with the name of every last rock, twig and weed we passed. And in Latin, no less! I promise you, ma'am, I feel decidedly ill-used. When we began the walk, I had no idea I was to be enlightened along the way. Why, I might as well have stayed at Cambridge."

His remark brought a crack of laughter from the older lady. "I assure you, sir, you will thank me for this instruction when you are older."

"It is a mystery to me," the young man said, "why

one's parents and teachers must end every boring lesson, and every reprimand, by averring that one will thank them in later years. First of all, if they are to be *my* later years, chances are none of you will be around to thank. In all probability, you will have been put to bed with a shovel, the lot of you!"

"Disrespectful pup!" Miss Evangeline admonished between laughs. "I shall strive to ignore that distasteful reference to my demise, and inform you . . ."

Spying Janine and Vincent, she stopped midsentence. "Janine, my love! Well met." Then, in a slightly cooler tone, "And Vincent."

The lady's sharp eyes took in her young friend's flushed face and slightly mussed hair, but she chose to ignore both circumstances for the moment. "I see we were all of one mind, to come down to enjoy the sunset reflected in the pond. A glorious sight, is it not, Vincent?"

"Yes, ma'am," he replied, making her an abbreviated bow. After giving the awe-inspiring splash of color a cursory look, he turned to his young cousin. "Actually, Gareth, I came looking for you."

The young gentleman stepped forward, obviously pleased to be sought out by his hero. "You were looking for me?"

"Yes. In light of what almost happened at the fair today, I believe we should stand guard at the entrance gates tonight."

The blue eyes shown with pleasure. "A good idea, sir. Will you take the first watch? Or shall I?"

The gentlemen agreed between them that their duties as keepers of the gate need not commence until nightfall, so they filled the next two hours by joining the ladies and partaking of the evening meal. And though Mr. Henley might be pleased to have been asked to share with his cousin the responsibility of standing watch, he did not let the possibility of future interlopers diminish his present enjoyment of the food, for like most gentlemen of his tender years, he was always hungry. Nor was he derelict in upholding his end of the dinner conversation, for there was much with which he wished to regale his companions regarding his day's adventures.

"It was all a sham," he said, brandishing his fork as if to emphasize his disappointment regarding a certain creature he had chanced to see at the fair. "In my entire life I was never so taken in."

"Are you telling us," Miss Craven said, managing, somehow, to keep a somber countenance, "that the animal was not a unicorn?"

"Ha! I daresay you will find it difficult to credit, ma'am, but I paid four pence to view a nanny goat with a bull's horn tied to her forehead."

At that, the young man's three auditors burst into laughter.

"A fool and his money," Vincent said, shaking his head at his gullible relative.

"Laugh if you wish, Cousin, for I daresay I appear the veryest Jack Pudding for paying money to see a unicorn, but I believe that even you would have parted with the necessary groat for a glimpse of the fellow in the next show. Half man and half horse! Only think of it!"

He paused long enough to consume a large forkful of chicken. "You will understand how barbarous the creature appeared, ladies, when I tell you that the placard alone was enough to send a group of milkmaids running in terror from the spot."

"But not you," Vincent remarked dryly.

"I should jolly well think not! To see such a remarkable creature, I was prepared to expend four pence and more."

Janine sought refuge behind her napkin, lest she laugh again.

"Unfortunately," Gareth continued with a sigh, "I was obliged to leave the fair before that particular show commenced."

While the conversation continued along this line, Janine tried to recall if she had ever spent a more pleasant evening. Though the meal was not on a grand scale—a fricasseed chicken, boiled vegetables, and a trifle drizzled over with a brandy sauce—she could find fault with neither the food nor the company.

Not that she tasted a single morsel that passed her lips. She was much too enchanted by the memory of what had passed between her and Vincent earlier at the pond. All she could think of were the gentle kisses he had trailed across her cheek, and the way his lips had brushed against hers, setting her very soul on fire.

A year or so ago, while she was still with Cousin Hortense, Janine had more or less resigned herself to the idea that she would live out her life without ever knowing love. Of course, she had known that marriage was out of the question even before she joined her cousin in Bath.

Three days after her father's death, when the will had been read, Janine had discovered that there was nothing left of the estate but the house and the land, both of which were entailed. What had become of the modest fortune her mother had brought to the family upon her marriage, no one knew. Sir George had lost it somehow. It was all gone, even the portion that should have come to Janine upon her wedding.

How and why the funds were lost was unimportant. The devastating truth was that she was portionless. And without a dowry, she had no chance of contracting an eligible alliance. No gentleman, no matter how enamored he might be of a lady, would offer his hand without at least a token dowry; not unless the prospective groom was a man of such wealth that he had no need to add to his coffers.

Though Janine knew that such wealthy men existed, in her impoverished state, she had about as much chance of meeting such a person as she had of sprouting wings and taking flight. Less, actually, for there was always the hope of angel's wings in the hereafter.

Actually, reconciling herself to the idea that she would never marry had proven much easier than resigning herself to a life without love, even though the possibility of finding someone she might feel a partiality for, and one who would reciprocate her feelings, had grown less likely with each month she remained with her cousin. However, it was only in the last year that she had begun to despair of ever meeting that special someone.

And now, here was Vincent.

Just looking across the table at him made Janine's pulse race. The idea that he might, at some later time, take her in his arms and kiss her again set the pulse to beating wildly. How she longed for that moment.

In a more perfect world, she would have been allowed to give in to her feelings, to walk around to the other side of the table and throw herself into Vincent's arms. Unfortunately, this world was not even close to being perfect, so she continued to sit quietly, her hands in her lap. "In my next life," she muttered.

"I beg your pardon," Gareth said. "I did not quite hear what you said."

Janine felt her face grow warm. She could not credit that she had actually spoken aloud. "I—er—did not mean to interrupt your conversation, sir. Please, do continue."

"Not at all, ma'am. I won nothing at the dart booth in any case, so my story is ended. I should much rather hear what you were saying about your next life."

"It was but a private jest, sir. I had no notion I had given voice to it."

"But you—"

"Give over, Gareth," Vincent said, "for Miss Morgan will not be coerced. I had it from her own lips, not twenty-four hours ago, that obedience goes against the grain with her. Furthermore," he added with a sardonic lift of one dark eyebrow, "I should warn you that she has a violent streak."

Ignoring his cousin's surprised expression, Vincent turned upon the recalcitrant lady a smile so sweet she fancied she could taste it.

"However," he continued, "I will admit to a certain curiosity myself. I had no notion, ma'am, that you espoused such radical views as multiple lives. Certainly it is an extraordinary belief to discover in any English miss, but especially so in a female who had to be *persuaded* into visiting a fortune-teller."

Gareth whistled. "You had your fortune told? By Jove! I wish I had done that. What did the seer predict for you, ma'am?"

Unwilling to tell anyone about the mysterious lover—the man with Vincent's face—Janine made up a story, adding to its color by waving her hands dramatically around her cup and peering into it, as though it were a crystal ball.

"I shall be rrrich," she said, rolling her "r" in imitation of the fortune-teller's heavy accent. "Rrrich beyond my wildest drrreams. And I shall visit exotic lands and see many rrrare and wondrrrous sights."

"Unicorns?" Vincent suggested. His tone was dry, but a quiver at the corners of his mouth betrayed him.

"But of courrrse. Herds of them."

He chuckled. "Surely you mean *herrrds* of them."

"Yes. Thank you for corrrecting me."

"Not at all. Happy to oblige. Was there more to this prophecy?"

"Only the parrrt about my powerrrs. On my forrrti-eth birrrthday, I shall become omnipotent."

"Forty?" Vincent asked, a devilish light in his eyes. "Thank goodness. That gives us a full year to do what we can to stop you."

Trying not to laugh, Janine stretched out her arm and pointed her finger at him, as if to administer a curse. "Those who would insult me, them I shall turrrn into slimy toads."

"There, you see," Vincent said, "I told you she had a violent streak."

"I should feel myself remiss in my duty as your friend," Miss Evangeline said, "if I did not tell you what is on my mind. Nay, what is troubling my heart."

The two ladies sat quite near the kitchen fireplace. Save for Jezebel, who reposed upon the mantel, they were alone for the first time since they had arrived at Morgan House. Vincent had taken the first watch down at the entrance gates, and Gareth had gone to his room in the carriage house to write the promised letter to his parents. As for Chloe, that good woman was uncharacteristically absent.

"I asked Chloe to leave us," Miss Evangeline said, "so that we might speak freely."

At the sound of her old friend's voice, Janine was reminded, for one fleeting moment, of Cousin Hortense. "Are you about to ring a peal over me?" she asked.

"Not over you, my love. Over myself. After all, it was I who insisted we come back to Morgan House. To your every protest, I turned a deaf ear. Now, it behooves me to do what I can to make amends for my interference, and for any repercussions that may have accrued from forcing you to return to this house."

Remembering Vincent's discourse at the pond, Janine wondered if everyone on the place was suffering from a case of self-recrimination. "Believe me, ma'am, you have nothing for which to make amends."

The older lady sighed. "I hope that may prove to be true. What concerns me, my love, is that in bringing you back to this house, I have forced you into a familiarity with Mr. . . . with Vincent, that might not have been altogether wise."

"But, ma'am. I thought you liked him."

"I do. He is intelligent without being one of those bores who must constantly parade their knowledge; he has an easy, teasing way about him that I find particularly amusing; and he is as handsome as he can stare. And though he is not so much a rogue as Zach Flynn, nonetheless, I like him very well."

"Then I do not see what—"

"The problem is not how much *I* may like Vincent. What concerns me in this matter is *your* sentiments. I could not but notice the way he teased you earlier. Nor the way you responded. Though you were in company, it appeared almost a *private* jest between you."

Her friend was quite right, it was a private joke, and as such, unseemly when others were present. "Your pardon, Miss Evangeline, I did not mean to—"

"Never mind that now, for it is neither here nor there." She sighed, as if wishing she might avoid what she was about to say. "Without further round-aboutation, I must ask you, my love, have you formed an attachment for this man?"

Janine had asked herself that question a million times since they returned from the pond. To her surprise, the answer had been the same each time. A resounding *yes*. "And if I have formed an attachment, would that be such a bad thing?"

"My dear child, surely you have not forgotten what is owed your family name. Not that I censure you overmuch for the confusion of your sentiments; that culpability I lay entirely at your father's feet. As many in the neighborhood could tell you, Sir George was much too democratic in his views. If it had been otherwise, the friendship between your brother and Zach Flynn would not have been allowed to continue past childhood."

Miss Evangeline rested her head against the back of her chair, her eyes closed. "You are a gentleman's daughter, and as such, any alliance between you and Vincent would be totally ineligible."

Leaning forward, Janine caught the older lady's hands in hers, forcing her to open her eyes so that she might read their expression. "Why is that, ma'am? You are a gentleman's daughter, yet you said yourself that Vincent is intelligent, and that you liked him."

"I beg you, child, do not give me back my words. I am old enough to be the man's mother, and the difference in our ages makes any friendship between us unexceptional. The same cannot be said for you, however. It simply will not do for you to be on terms of familiarity with Vincent."

"Why not?"

Miss Evangeline had the grace to blush. "Because he and Zach have more in common than the similitude of their faces. I fear that he, like Zach, is a bastard."

A bastard.

Though the harsh word echoed inside Janine's brain, it came as no surprise to her. After all, Chloe had hinted as much that very afternoon, and Janine had already speculated upon the possibility that Vincent might be a love child. Hearing Miss Evangeline actually give voice to the word made it seem more real, but it did not make it, or its object, distasteful.

"The circumstances of Vincent's birth are a matter of unimportance," Janine said. "He is a wonderful man, and that is enough for me. I do not care whose name he bears."

Miss Evangeline chose not to credit the sincerity of the younger lady's arguments. "That is your heart speaking, my love, when you would do better to listen to your head. No good can come of such a misalliance. Vincent is a man with little but his charm to recommend him, while you are—"

"I disagree, ma'am. Vincent has much to recommend him. He is a man of honorable character and loyalty, and he—"

"I stand corrected. What I meant to say was that no matter how numerous his finer qualities, they are not sufficient to render him eligible as a husband, at least not for the daughter of Sir George Morgan, Baronet."

"For all the good that particular distinction has done me! I may be a gentleman's daughter, but look at me dispassionately, ma'am, for I am a woman no longer in her first blush of youth. Moreover, I am alone in the world, penniless, and without promise of future employment. So I would ask you, my friend, which of those aforementioned attributes would most recommend me as an acceptable bride for some gentleman's son?"

The question being unanswerable, Miss Evangeline chose to say nothing, and after a few minutes of strained silence, Janine excused herself and went in search of a breath of fresh air. To her regret, fresh air was all she found, for Vincent had already walked down to the gate to stand guard against possible intrusion by Cal and the mob from the fair.

And though she wished she might stroll down the carriageway to visit with him, she knew she should not. It did not matter that she and he had already spent a night alone in the house, unchaperoned; if she should seek him out now, Miss Evangeline would be scandalized. Janine might disagree with the lady, but she had no wish to offend her only friend in this world.

Not, of course, that she meant to follow that good woman's advice!

Janine had no intention of keeping her distance from Vincent. Far from it. She loved him, and no considerations of class or legitimacy would stop her from being with him. Not if he loved her too.

Whoever or whatever Vincent was, she wanted to spend the rest of her life with him. And if he would have her, that was exactly what she meant to do.

Chapter 12

I should not have touched her!

Angry with himself, Vincent abandoned his place beside the wrought-iron entrance gate that hung drunkenly, its lynch pin obviously lost for some time, and followed the meandering of the low stone wall. Walking at a sharp pace, he traveled for some distance down the road, its rutted surface lit by the golden-white light of a full moon. After frightening more than one small creature into scurrying beneath the thick hedgerows, he turned and retraced his steps, having found no relief from his anger.

Unable to free his consciousness of her image, her laugh, the clean, fresh smell of her hair, or anything about her, he cursed aloud, calling himself a fool. "You should never have touched her!"

That was his first mistake, of course, reaching out and running his hand along the soft, disturbingly feminine contour of her jaw. If he had kept his distance, he never would have experienced the satin smoothness of her skin, skin that begged to be caressed again and again. Or if he had kept a tighter rein upon his desire once he had touched her, he would have been able to control the hunger that led him to take her in his arms.

Taking her in his arms, that had been his greatest mistake! For if he had not felt the softness of her lips, and tasted the sweet innocence of her first kiss, he would not now be wishing with all his soul that he might hold her once again, to mold her soft pliant body against his, and kiss her as he had longed to kiss her this afternoon.

While cursing himself for not keeping his passion under control, he thanked all the powers that be for the timely arrival of his cousin and Miss Craven. Janine deserved better than him—better than Satan's spawn. Vincent knew that, even if she did not. She deserved someone who knew how to love with a free heart. Vincent Thornton did not possess that knack, and if he had ever learned it, his father and the cane fields had beaten it out of him years ago.

With Janine's beauty, her intelligence, her wit, she could find a man worthy of her; make a good marriage. She needed only the opportunity.

And Vincent could give her that opportunity.

All that was necessary was a respectable dowry and a sponsor. With his wealth, the former would be a simple matter. To obtain the latter, he need only enlist the aid of Gareth's mother.

If his aunt would agree to take Janine under her wing, and perhaps plan a trip with her to Town, or to one of the fashionable watering places, a suitable match was a certainty. Aunt Letitia need only introduce Janine to a few gentlemen whose hearts were whole and unscarred, and the young lady's vivacity would do the rest. Any man must find her all that was appealing and desirable in a wife.

Yes. There was the solution.

As soon as he returned to London, he would write to his aunt with his proposal. And though the very thought of Janine married to another man seemed to reach inside Vincent's body and rip out every last one of his vital organs, he cast aside his feelings of loss and began to compose the letter in his head.

It was while he mentally listed the lady's many virtues that he heard footfalls upon the road.

"Who is there?" he demanded, carefully withdrawing the pistol he had tucked inside his coat. "Show yourself, and be quick about it, for I should regret shooting an innocent person."

Someone stepped from the shadows into a pool of moonlight. The figure wore a dark cloak, with the hood pulled down low, obscuring the face. Since the night was pleasantly balmly, Vincent suspected that the cloak had been worn more for its concealing properties than for its warmth.

"Do not shoot," came a soft voice. "It is Franny. And I am alone."

Franny Aylesworth hugged herself inside the dark cloak she wore, as if chilled by what she had heard. "I don't believe it," she said.

"Perhaps," Vincent said, not unkindly, "you only *wish* not to believe it."

"No. Zach isn't capable of such a cruel deed. He's not a coward, but fighting isn't his style. He is much more likely to talk himself out of a dispute than he is to resort to violence. I suppose that is a result of all the mills he endured while still a lad. 'Tis a wonder he grew to be so handsome, for he was forever nursing a black eye or a bruised jaw." Her voice grew angry. "You will not believe how cruel other lads can be to a boy without a father."

"I can imagine," Vincent said softly.

"Perhaps you can," she said, a note of compassion in her voice. "But be that as it may, my Zach would never do what you accuse him of. He would not beat up on a defenseless young man, nor would he skulk in some alley like a common criminal, waiting to commit the dirty deed."

"Even if you are correct," Vincent said, his tone skeptical, "and Flynn is the man of peace you believe him to be, what of the young man's other accusation? Is *your Zach* of too pure a heart to cheat?"

"Ha! As though he needed to fuzz the deck to win. No one can best him at cards. You have only to ask around; anyone will tell you that I speak the truth. His skill is so well known in the neighborhood, that nobody will give him a game. That is why he needed to go to Town."

At this last revelation, she clamped her hand over her mouth, as if to stop the words.

"So. You admit that Zach was in London."

She bit her lip, then slowly nodded her head, the blond tresses as memorable by moonlight as by sunlight.

"But it was all Sir Burton's idea! He was the one who came looking for Zach. Him with his schemes. Said his plan could not fail. Ha! I never liked him—even when he was a boy—for he gives my Zach ideas above his station. Whenever he's around, Zach imitates him, begins to act and talk like some Town swell."

"And the plan?" Vincent asked, not wanting to let her get too far off the subject.

"Sir Burton is badly dipped, as the saying goes, but he said there were a few paintings left at Morgan House he could sell. Once he sold the paintings, his plan was to supply Zach with a set of fancy Town clothes and enough money to make sure he was accepted into the places where the play is high. They were to split the winnings."

She dashed her hand across her cheeks, as though brushing away tears. "We were to sail to America on our share of the take. Get away from here, and have a chance at a new start. Zach promised that if we had enough money left over after we booked passage, we could use it to buy a piece of land, for a farm of our own. He was over there with the army, don't you know, and he says there's thousands of miles of unsettled land in America."

"So I have heard."

"And Zach says there are thick forests as far as the eye can see, and soil so rich a person's only got to throw a few seeds at it, then sit back and wait for the crops to push out of the ground."

Not wanting to shatter all her dreams in one night, Vincent chose to keep his tongue between his teeth on the subject of American agricultural possibilities. "Perhaps you can still go there."

"Not if you have him arrested," she replied, the enthusiasm gone from her voice.

"Of course you can. Even if Zach is found guilty, he would probably have to serve no more than six years."

"Six years! I can't wait that long."

"Of course you can. It is not so very long. You are what . . . nineteen? Twenty? You would only be twenty-six when—"

"I tell you, I can't. My father says if Zach don't marry me before my next birthday, then I got to take Phineas McFee, or one of the other lads."

She pulled the cloak around her as though suddenly chilled. "Fa says he's fed me long enough, and he don't plan to do it one more minute past my birthday. If I am not married by then, he says he'll throw me out."

Vincent knew better than to suggest that the smithy was in jest. If Cal was a bully, chances are he learned the behavior at home, watching the example of his father.

Swallowing the profanity that sprang to his lips, Vincent said simply, "I am sorry, Franny."

"Sorry won't do me a bit of good if—"

"You all right, Cousin?" Gareth called from a shadowed spot near the gate. "I have a pistol primed and ready if you are not."

"I am fine," he answered, "but I am pleased you had the foresight to ask before you revealed your presence. Put the pistol away, then come out and meet Miss Franny. Though you saw her earlier, at the fair, there was no time then for introductions."

When the young man joined them, his hands were bare of weaponry. "Did not really have a barker," he said, the blush on his handsome face evident in the moonlight. "Just thought I should sound a bit more prepossessing if I said I did."

"Very wise," Vincent remarked, keeping his tone bland, then he made his relative known to Franny. After the introductions were completed, he asked the lad if he would bring Amigo around and take Miss Franny back to the village.

"No need to put the gentleman to the bother," she said. "It's but three miles."

Since neither gentleman would hear of her walking those three miles alone, Gareth did as his cousin bid him, and went to fetch the horse. In a matter of minutes he was astride the gelding, with the girl sitting snugly behind him. "Be careful," Vincent warned, "and if you see anyone, try to get off the road and hide."

"I know a way across the fields," Franny offered. "If we don't take the road, there won't be anybody to see us. And with this full moon, if we go slow, the horse shouldn't have any trouble finding good footing."

Her suggestion accepted, the two young people set off across the field, while Vincent stood in the road and watched their progress. Above the sound of a barn owl *hoo-hooing* in the distance, he heard Amigo's hoofbeats, muffled by a thick blanket of bluebells and growing fainter by the minute. When the night finally swallowed up both horse and riders, Vincent resumed his solitary guarding of the gate.

It was probably no more than an hour later when he heard other hoofbeats; only this time, they came from down the road. And since there was also a decided rattle of carriage wheels, Vincent stepped into the shadows to await the new arrival.

Within seconds the vehicle appeared. It was a green and yellow Stanhope pulled by a black gelding with a white blaze on his forehead—a showy, but obviously expensive animal. As for the driver of the equipage, he was a petulant-faced man of about twenty-eight years, and his rather plump form was encased in skin tight pantaloons, well-made Hessians, and a snug-fitting coat. The clothes, as well as the curly brim beaver, all bore the unmistakable stamp of the London artisan.

Certain this was not one of the villagers, Vincent set the lock of his pistol to full-cock, then stepped out into the open. "Halt!"

"What the deuce!" said the stranger, only just keeping his horse in check.

"Identify yourself," Vincent demanded, "before my finger grows restive and squeezes this trigger."

"The devil, you say! Why should I identify myself to some blackguard who waylays me on my own land?"

Momentarily taken aback, Vincent stared at the

man. Could this be Sir Burton Morgan? Though there was something vaguely familiar about the face—something that teased at his memory—Vincent could see no resemblance to Janine in that dissipated countenance.

"I did not ask about the land, sir, for I know to whom it belongs. It is your name I require."

For an answer, the man jerked sharply on the ribbons, causing the showy gelding to lay back his ears and snort in alarm. Receiving a second, even rougher jerk of the reins, the startled animal raised up on his hind legs, pawing the air with his front hooves.

Not wanting to become a casualty of those lethal appendages, Vincent backed out of the way, but to his surprise, his progress was checked after only a few steps. Someone, he had no idea who, pressed something cold and unyielding into the back of his neck. He had no difficulty in recognizing that object, it was the bore of a pistol.

Choosing to obey the greater of two threats, he remained perfectly still, realizing too late that the horseplay had been a ruse to keep him from hearing the stranger's accomplice coming around behind him.

"I'll take that barker," the man said, holding out his hand for Vincent's pistol. "We wouldn't want it to go off, now would we?"

Confident in the knowledge that his knife was in its sheath beneath his coat, Vincent surrendered the pistol without argument.

"You took your sweet time," the driver accused, bringing his horse under control once again.

"Patience," replied his accomplice affably, "is one of those virtues we would all do well to embrace."

"Deuce take it, man, if you spout another platitude at me, I vow I shall be tempted to put paid to your existence."

The man with the pistol merely laughed. "You're a lover, Burt, not a murderer."

Burt! So it was true. This was, indeed, Janine's brother. And if he was Sir Burton, then it must follow that his loquacious companion was none other than the bogus baron.

The driver swore. "Never mind what I am, you blasted jaw-me-dead. Five full days I have endured your endless palaver, and at this moment, the only thing I wish to hear from you is what we are to do with this fellow now that we have caught him."

"I suppose," answered his accomplice, "we have no choice but to take him up to the house and see if we can discover who he is."

The kitchen was unoccupied. Vincent assumed the ladies had retired for the night, for the candles on the table and those on the mantel had been extinguished, and the fire banked for safety. Still, there was enough light to see how to move about the room without stumbling into the furniture. Not waiting for instructions, he moved over to the fireplace and sought the phosphorous box.

"Here," Sir Burton said, "what are you doing there? Desist, I say."

"I am lighting a candle," he said, continuing as though the owner of the house had not spoken. Vincent had allowed himself to be urged up the carriageway at pistol point, more to listen in upon his captors' conversation than for any other consideration, but now he had had enough. "I wish to see your faces," he said. "I believe I have earned that right."

"What cheek! Look here, you. You will move away from there this instant, or I shall—"

"You will what?" The words were softly spoken, but the authority behind them was not lost on the other two occupants of the room.

In the silence that followed, Vincent lit the candle, lifted it from the mantel, and walked toward Sir Burton. He held the light aloft so that he might satisfy himself about the gentleman's appearance, and as he did so, he realized why the face seemed so familiar; he had seen it before, in London. This was the man who had accosted him on the street a week ago, the intoxicated fellow who had caught hold of his coat sleeve, babbling on about *the plan*, and about how well it was working and how they would soon be rich as Croesus.

Needing only one further piece of evidence to be satisfied as to the identity of the men who had cheated, then savagely beaten, young Mr. Neville, Vincent turned toward the taller, slimmer man, the man who still held the pistol.

"So," he said, after perusing the chiseled features, the jet-black hair, and the amber—eyes eerily like his father's—"'tis true. *Satan* spawned another. And this one molded even more in his image than am I. You, I collect, are the bogus baron."

"Zach Flynn," he replied, making Vincent a mocking bow, "at your service. I suppose I need not ask your name."

Sir Burton shoved aside one of the chairs at the table, making it fall back upon the stone floor, the noise sounding overloud in the quiet that had followed Zach Flynn's comment. "Well, I jolly well intend to hear his name, and quite soon, for I have no notion who this fellow may be. Furthermore, I resent some Captain Queer-nabs walking into *my* house as though he owned the place, acting like a damned duke, and shoving a light in my face, bold as brass! I have a good mind to take my crop to the fellow. Teach him how to behave when in the presence of his betters."

"Stubble it, Burt. Can't you see who this is?"

"Odsbodikins!" he replied, his face becoming red with anger. "Am I expected to know every vagabond who—"

"Just look at him! Do not be misled by the clothes and the beard. Notice the eyes."

Though taking his cohort's instructions in bad part, Sir Burton did as he was bid, looking carefully at Vincent's eyes. "I cannot see anything especially . . ." The remark seemed to hang in the air, unfinished, for Vincent had removed his hat, revealing his straight, black hair.

Sir Burton's plump face paled from red to pasty white. "You!"

"Just so," Vincent said.

"What . . . what are you doing here? How did you—"

"Did you think I would not come? Surely you were not so naive as to believe you could destroy my name and my reputation and not suffer the consequences?"

Trembling so badly he was unable to stand, Sir Burton sought one of the chairs at the table and more or less fell into it. With a shudder, he propped his elbows upon the freshly scrubbed wood and buried his face in his hands.

When his friend said nothing, Zach stepped forward. "We meant you no harm, you know. Just a few hands of cards, that was all we planned. I would sit in on a game or two with men who could afford to lose, then after winning some money, I would disappear, with no one hurt and no one the wiser."

"Ah," Vincent said, "but someone did get hurt, did they not?"

Sir Burton looked up then, his eyes haunted, his skin resembling unkneaded dough. "That was none of our doing! Why, it was Zach and I who chased the ruffians away and put young Neville into a hackney to be taken to his home. Even paid the jarvey from my own pocket. You must believe me, Thornton, we had nothing to do with the young man's injuries."

"Then why did you run? If you are so blameless, why did you not see young Neville home? If you had stayed to explain the whole, *I* would not now stand accused of the deed."

"We . . . we did not know you would be accused. Acquit us of that, at least. But we could not stay, for if we had, we might have been obliged to return the money we had won."

"The money!" Vincent all but spat the words.

Sir Burton sat up, his expression indignant. "Easy for you to come all highty-tighty over us, you with all your blunt. You inherited a king's ransom, so how could you possibly understand my troubles? You have never known what it is to do without . . . to watch other men with stables full of horses, while you must make do with only one. But I have! And now the duns are after me like a pack of wolves, demanding payment for—"

"Save your breath, Burt."

"But I want him to know. Rich men have no idea how the rest of us must live. Only consider how we have been obliged to hole-up in that disgusting ale house, with half the village wishful of blaming you for that thwarted robbery, and—"

"Enough, Burt! Can't you see that his lordship doesn't want to hear about our problems? Lord Thornton has already decided—"

All three men heard the gasp that came from the shadows near the larder door. The soft, feminine sound could not have intruded upon the conversation more if it had been a cannon shot.

Holding up the candle, Vincent peered into the shadows. "Janine? Is that you?"

She came forward then, seemingly unmindful of her bare feet, or of the hair that tumbled about her shoulders in glorious disarray. Obviously roused from her bed, she had taken only enough time to throw an old fringed shawl around her shoulders to cover her white lawn night rail.

"Vincent," she said, walking directly to him and looking up into his eyes, her own beautiful orbs wide with shock and disbelief. "It is not true, is it? Tell me you are not a lord."

Sir Burton saw fit to answer the request, apparently not at all surprised to see his sister. "Of course it is true, my girl. Do not be a looby. Who did you think he was?"

She did not answer her brother, but continued to stare at Vincent. "Are you a peer?" she asked, the words barely above a whisper.

Vincent nodded. "When I first arrived here in Bexham, I thought it important that I retain my anonymity, for I had no notion who I might encounter. Believe me, once I came to know you, I wanted to tell you the truth. You will never know how much I disliked deceiving you, but I—"

"But you deceived me nonetheless."

When Vincent would have spoken, she shook her head. "Please," she said, her voice flat and devoid of emotion, "spare me your belated confidences. I suppose I was laughably easy to fool. How amused you must have been, making cakes of us all. And not just me, but Miss Evangeline and Chloe as well."

"Miss Craven is here?" Sir Burton asked. "Well, sister, at least you were not so lost to propriety as to stay here alone with his lordship, laying yourself open to all manner of tittle-tattle. When I looked out the window of the alehouse this morning and saw you standing at the bridge, with a man, your arm in his, I feared that you might have—"

"Propriety?"

Slowly Janine turned to face her brother, anger vying with despair for dominance within her. "Did you say *propriety*, Burton? I vow, the word sits ill upon your lips. In fact, I wonder that it does not stick in your throat and choke you."

"I say, old girl! No need for name calling. Try to remember that I am head of the family, and as such, deserving of respect."

"That which you *deserve* may be much closer than you know. As for respect, there is not a man in this room worthy of such. Liars, all three of you. And I should not be surprised if the lot of you . . ."

The hollow clink of horseshoes sounded upon the stone walkway just outside the kitchen, distracting Janine and causing her to suspend her animadversions upon the characters of her three auditors. While everyone turned toward the partially open door, Amigo's proud head appeared in the opening, then he pushed his way inside the room.

Sir Burton was the first to react. "What the devil! Is my house turned into a stable, that cattle amble in at will?"

Vincent rushed to the chestnut, who whickered nervously. He still wore his saddle, but of the rider, there was no sign.

"*¿Que pasa?*" he muttered, catching hold of the bridle and running a calming hand along the horse's neck. "Where is Gareth?"

"Here," came the faint reply.

The young man staggered to the door, clutching the jamb to keep from falling to the floor. His coat was covered in dirt, with the sleeve torn at the shoulder, and both his cravat and his handsome face were spattered with blood. His left eye was already beginning to swell shut, and his lower lip showed a deep gash that was bleeding profusely.

Janine and Zach Flynn both rushed forward to offer the lad their support, each taking an arm and helping him over to the table where he collapsed into one of the chairs.

"Cousin?" Gareth said, raising his head enough to look at Zach Flynn, then blinking as if to clear his vision. "Your beard. When did you shave?"

Vincent backed the gelding out of the kitchen, then went to his cousin, kneeling down before the young man and taking him gently by the shoulders. "Gareth? Can you hear me, lad?"

"I . . . I hear."

"Who did this to you?" he asked, the words so icy Janine felt as though a shock of cold air had blasted its way beneath her shawl.

"You put Miss Franny into my keeping," Gareth replied, his breathing labored. "You trusted me. Told me to see her safely home."

Zach Flynn stepped forward then. "Franny? What about Franny? Where is she? Is she hurt?"

Vincent aimed a quelling look at the man before returning his attention to Gareth.

"Yes, I trusted you. I still do, lad. Nothing has happened to change my mind. But tell me how you were injured."

"He slapped her. Knocked her to the ground. Could not let him do so and not answer for it. Had to stop him from—"

"Who?" Vincent repeated, an angry muscle jerking in his jaw. "Who did this?"

"Cal. He was waiting at the bridge. Not up to his weight, of course, but I had to defend Miss Franny. At least, I had to try. Had to make him . . ." The final words were nearly inaudible, and after a deep breath that made the young man grimace and clasp his hand against his ribs, he moaned and slumped forward, his blond head falling against his cousin's broad shoulder.

Holding his young relative so he did not fall, Vincent stood. The expression on his face was as hard and unyielding as granite, but he lifted the lad in his arms with infinite care. "May I use your room?" he asked Janine.

Without waiting for her reply, he turned and walked toward the housekeeper's bedroom, the familiarity of the act not lost upon the young lady's brother.

Chapter 13

Hearing the light tapping at the bedroom door, Janine left the injured lad in the capable hands of Miss Craven and Chloe and went to see who had been so thoughtless as to disturb them.

"What do you want?" she asked, opening the door and slipping outside.

Before he spoke, Vincent reached behind her and closed the door. His hair was mussed, as though he had raked his hands through it numerous times, and his mouth was set in a harsh line, fatigue or worry etching little grooves at the corners.

"How is he?" he asked, the words almost a whisper.

"Sleeping," she replied, keeping her voice quiet as well. "Fortunately, Chloe had some laudanum, and she managed to get Mr. Henley to swallow a few drops before she sewed up the cut to his lip."

Janine swallowed, still sickened by the memory of the young gentleman's injuries. "Chloe is a notable needlewoman, so the wound should heal nicely, and leave little or no scar."

"And his ribs?"

"Miss Evangeline thinks one of them may be cracked. Otherwise, there is no permanent damage. She and Chloe bandaged Mr. Henley securely, and he seemed much more comfortable afterward."

Upon hearing the prognosis, Vincent sighed, and his entire body seemed to relax with the gesture. Observing him, Janine only just managed to stop herself from reaching out to brush a lock of hair back from his forehead.

"And you are certain he is sleeping, and not unconscious?"

"Quite certain. Before Miss Evangeline let Chloe give him the laudanum, she asked him several questions, just to assure herself that his mind was clear."

"What kind of questions?"

"For the most part, they concerned Alexander the Great. When he was born, his greatest victory, that sort of thing."

Momentarily taken aback, Vincent raised an eyebrow. "And the lad was able to answer such questions lucidly?"

Janine nodded. "Miss Evangeline seemed well satisfied with his responses, with the exception of something she quoted in Latin. Apparently, your cousin attributed to Pliny the Elder a remark that should have been credited to Pliny the Younger, and my friend, the instructress, bid him brush up on his history before he returned to Cambridge."

"Bless her," Vincent said. "A very cool-headed lady is Miss Craven."

"I am pleased that you think so. You might, however, be interested to hear your cousin's views upon the matter."

At his look of interest, Janine continued. "Just before the drops took effect, Mr. Henley informed Miss Evangeline that her questions had very likely given him a fever of the brain. 'These curst bandages I can endure,' he told her, 'but I am far too injured to tolerate Latin.'"

Vincent smiled suddenly, and that smile was like

the first real spring day after a cold winter—totally unexpected, but sublimely warm and infinitely welcome. Presented with such an overpowering stimulus, it was no wonder that Janine found her own lips turning up in response to his.

But when his gaze fastened upon her mouth for several moments before traveling to her eyes, his gray orbs holding hers, almost as if seeking the answer to a question, she was obliged to harden her heart against him. Two hours ago she would have been thrilled at such a gaze, happy to answer any of his questions— spoken or not—but that was before she had learned that he was Baron Thornton.

Earlier in the evening, when she had believed him to be the nameless by-blow of some unknown Londoner, she had been ready to defy the conventions and enter into a misalliance, if that was his wish. Because she loved him, she had been willing to ignore the question of his legitimacy. At that time, she had been convinced that if he loved her, too, nothing could stop them from being together.

Now, of course, she knew better.

In one instant, everything had changed. Vincent was no longer just the hard-working, wonderful, caring man who had teased her, and kissed her, and made her long for more of the same. Now he was a person of noble lineage—a peer with a long-established title and vast wealth. A man far above her touch.

Though Janine's democratic notions—as Miss Evangeline had called them—might have prompted her to marry a man who was her social inferior, she was not such a fool as to believe that a wealthy baron—a true matrimonial prize by London, or any other, standards—would wish to align himself with a penniless, country nobody.

By acknowledging this truth, if only to herself, she put paid to her previous fanciful notions of traveling life's road with Vincent. The fortune-teller had predicted that Janine would not undertake the journey alone, but she had said nothing about that person "whose heart beats in harmony with your own," being a wealthy peer.

Looking at him now, with that heart-stopping smile easing the harsh line of his mouth and obliterating the little grooves etched at the corners, she was obliged to remind herself that she must give over thinking of him. Give over for all time. Vincent—nay, Lord Thornton—could look as high as he liked for a bride; he could choose from among any of the young ladies at Almack's. And though the very idea of his offering his hand to some *other* lady caused a sadness to settle inside Janine's chest, robbing her of needed air, she managed to conceal the fact.

"I must go," she said, "Miss Evangeline may need me."

When she would have turned and retreated to the relative privacy of the bedroom, Vincent forestalled her by reaching out and catching a thick lock of her hair, where it rested on her shoulder.

"I am glad you did not put it up again," he said, the words spoken so softly Janine doubted if she had truly heard them.

Like one mesmerized, she stood very still while he rested the tress upon his open palm, as though weighing it.

"A man could lose himself in such hair," he said, "for it is as rich and dark and warm as the earth itself, yet it shines like the stars."

Slowly he turned his hand, winding the thick strand around it, and focusing his attention upon the silken locks. "Once before, my friend, you gave me your trust, even though I had done nothing to merit it. It was a gift, and I treasured it more than I can say. Now, without it, I find I am bereft. And though you have every reason to doubt my sincerity, I beg you will give me your trust again. I make you my promise, you will not regret it."

Janine's heart wanted to cry out, "Yes! Yes!" but her mind bid her say him Nay. When she tried to speak, the words would not come.

After several moments—moments in which Vincent searched her face—he relaxed his hand and let the strand of hair slip through his fingers.

"I see," he said.

Stepping back, he made her a rather formal bow. "I quite understand your reticence. Faith is like a piece of fine porcelain; though it is capable of lasting a lifetime, even through the roughest handling, once it is broken, it is almost impossible to mend."

He lifted her hand and brought it to his lips for the briefest of salutes. "I pray that one day you will find it in your heart to forgive me."

Not waiting for a reply, he turned and walked away, his steps quick and purposeful. It was only after he had passed through the kitchen and closed the heavy wooden door behind him that Janine found her voice.

"Vincent! Wait! I . . ."

While she stared at the hand that was still warm from Vincent's kiss, wanting with all her heart to run after him and tell him that she had not lost faith in him, Sir Burton seemed to materialize from out of the shadows.

"He will return," he said.

Startled to discover that she was not alone, Janine jumped. "Have you taken to eavesdropping, Burton? It is not a habit I recommend. You would be wise to give it up, for I know from personal experience that one often hears things best left undiscovered."

"I could not help but overhear what passed between you and Lord Thornton," he replied. "And far from wishing myself ignorant of the circumstances, I am pleased to have discovered which way the wind blows."

Janine had no wish to discuss Vincent with her brother, so she favored him with a cold look meant to depress impertinence. "*Which way the wind blows?* I collect that is some sort of cant phrase. I do not know what it signifies, and let me assure you, I do not wish to be enlightened. Not unless it is your way of telling me that in the three years since I heard from you last, you have become a prognosticator of the weather."

Sir Burton was impervious to both her cold look and her sarcasm. "Do not be a pea goose, my girl. And do not think you can distract me with your nonsensical talk, for believe me, I have twigged the real story."

"*Twigged?* More cant, I suppose."

"Blast it, girl! Stop trying to divert me from my purpose. I saw what passed between you and his lordship. Glimmed it with my own eyes."

"No matter what you think you saw, Burton, I assure you it was—"

"Not but what I *now* wish you had not brought Miss Craven with you to play gooseberry. That was a mistake, for I feel certain that if you had been here alone with a fellow of Thornton's ilk, he would have managed to wheedle his way into your bed."

Nearly choked by outrage, Janine gasped, "How . . . how dare you!"

Ignoring her outburst, he continued. "And though I am not handy with my fives, if I had been fortunate enough to discover the two of you here alone, I am confident I could have prevailed upon his lordship to marry you. But I shall not repine over that squandered opportunity, for all may not be lost. If you will be led by me, I think you might yet find the man's wedding ring upon your finger."

"Sir! You go beyond the line of what is endurable."

"I see you have reservations, and I quite understand your sentiments. Under normal circumstances I would not be best pleased to see a sister of mine marry into such a family. How could I? Bad blood there, don't you know? The father was a complete rotter—known far and wide as *Satan*. And from what I hear, the son was such a young hell-hound that he was shipped off to foreign parts to complete his education."

Sir Burton patted her on the shoulder, lack of experience with such brotherly gestures causing his face to grow quite florid. "Not a true gentleman, you understand, but rich as Croesus."

Janine shrugged his hand away. "Of course," she said, breathing deeply in an attempt to control her anger, "since you are such a fine and honorable person yourself, you are the perfect judge of who is and who is not a true gentleman."

Finally noticing her ire, her brother blinked, as if unable to comprehend its source. "What did I—"

"As for my being led by you," she continued, "though I admit that it goes hard with me to ignore the wishes of a brother who has always put my welfare before his own—a brother who squandered his inheritance and allowed our home to deteriorate, becoming little better than a rat's nest—in this instance, I think I must heed the dictates of my own conscience."

"But . . . but this is our one chance to recoup the family fortune! And though I admit that I may not have been altogether wise in my handling of my inheritance, I promise to do better in the future. With but a little help, I could pay off my creditors, then I would restore the lands, the house, everything."

When she made no reply, he said, "We have before us an unparalleled opportunity to regain what was lost. You . . . you must see that. Surely you cannot mean to whistle this amazing piece of good luck down the wind."

Janine held up her finger, as if testing the direction of the wind, then she puckered her lips and whistled.

Sir Burton stared at her, incredulity writ upon his plump face. "Foolish, willful girl! Do you desire to see your only relative languishing in some filthy prison? I can only suppose that to be the case, for depend upon it, that is where I shall find myself if Lord Thornton takes me back to London."

"Ultimately, Burton, we must all take responsibility for our actions, so if you—"

"And what of yourself? Have you considered the hardships you will be obliged to endure if you are left an old maid?"

"If that is to be my fate, then I shall bear it as I have borne other deprivations."

"You cannot mean it! No, I know you do not. 'Tis too absurd."

Desperate to believe his own prophecy, he laughed, though the sound came out not the carefree display he had intended, but a nervous giggle. "You will come to your senses, my girl. I know you will. Only think of the pin money you would have, not to mention the jewels and the pretty folderols. Once you have had time to reflect upon the advantages of marrying a man as wealthy as Lord Thornton, I know you will reconsider, and give over this stubbornness."

Janine shook her head. "You must not delude yourself, Burton. Things will never be as you wish them, for I shall never be Lady Thornton."

She swallowed a rather large lump that had crept into her throat, the words as painful for her to say as they were for her brother to hear. "Nothing would induce me to marry Vincent. N-nothing."

As Vincent and Amigo approached the stone bridge just outside the village, he reined in the horse, obliged to wait while two revelers, their caps askew and their arms around one another's shoulders in drunken camaraderie, wove their way across the span. It being almost midnight, the fair-goers had departed long ago, and the few stragglers in evidence upon Bexham's high street were men who had remained behind to lift a pint or two with their friends at the tap room of the Red Hart Inn.

When the two inebriates finally drew near, Vincent asked them if they knew where he might find Cal Aylesworth.

"Find Cal?" said one, laughing, "didn't know he was lost."

"Too big to lose," agreed the other, slapping his knee and joining in the laughter.

Not wanting to prolong this interview, Vincent reached inside his coat and extracted two guineas, holding them aloft so the gold shone in the bright moonlight. "Tell me, have you seen Cal within the last hour?"

Suddenly serious, both men stepped close enough to ogle the coins.

"Aylesworth left the Red Hart some time ago," said the one, "bound for the smithy. Wanted his bed, like as not."

"Leave him till tomorrow," advised the other. "Cal can be a real mean fellow, he can. Best not to borrow trouble."

Vincent meant to do more than *trouble* the bully. He was resolved to make Cal rue the day he wreaked his vengeance upon a young man only just past his boyhood. Having learned all he needed to know, he tossed the guineas to the ground, and while the two men scrambled to retrieve the coins, he urged Amigo across the bridge and toward the high street, their destination Jem Aylesworth's blacksmith shop.

As he passed the boarded up alehouse, however, something near the rear of the ramshackle place caught his attention. It was a green and yellow Stanhope, and harnessed to the gig was a black gelding with a white blaze on his forehead. The ribbons had been looped over the limb of a willow tree, and the horse's head hung down as though he slept. Recognizing both horse and gig, and wondering how they came to be there, Vincent turned Amigo in that direction. He had not long to wait to satisfy his curiosity.

"I'll kill you for this, Flynn," said a rough voice from somewhere behind the derelict building. "You b'aint satisfied with getting me shot, now you've turned your hand to kidnapping. Holding a barker to a man's head while he's abed be just the kind of coward's act I'd expect from you."

"Just wanted a private word with you, Cal, old fellow," Zach Flynn replied pleasantly. "Nothing wrong with that."

Cal called him a vile name. "There's a private word for you."

"Sticks and stones, my man, sticks and stones. I've been called worse by better men than you. As for me getting you shot, it seems your memory is every bit as dull as your wits. As much as I would enjoy taking credit for the deed, the fault is all your own. 'Twas never my idea to rob that coach, and you and I both know it. You talked the lads into the robbery. All I did was give them a few pointers so they wouldn't get themselves killed."

So, on that score, at least, Flynn was innocent. For some reason, Vincent was pleased to learn that the man who looked so much like him was not totally without principles.

Not wanting to give away his presence too soon, Vincent led Amigo back around to the front of the building where he tied the gelding to a lone hawthorn bush. Then, staying low and close to the building— one of the tactics he had learned from the fierce Quaxiutl tribesmen of South America—he moved quietly toward the voices.

His first look at Cal Aylesworth was an eye-opener, for the man lived up to his reputation as a mountain. Noticeably taller than Vincent's six-foot-plus, he weighed at least seventeen stone, and every bit of it was solid muscle. His neck was as thick as the base of a small tree, and his hands, which were balled into fists and raised threateningly, were very nearly the size of hams.

"You're a spineless fish, Flynn! A chicken-hearted, weak-kneed coward. As well to give over the barker now, and save yourself a beating, 'cause you b'aint man enough to shoot me."

"He might not be," Vincent said quietly, stepping from the shadows into the moonlight, his arm raised and his pistol pointed directly at Cal's large, close-cropped head, "but I should have no more reservations about shooting you than I would have about ridding the world of a rabid dog."

"What the devil!" Cal looked from Vincent to Flynn, then back again. "I must've drunk more ale than I thought. Me peepers is seeing double. Else that bitch, Rose Flynn, dropped two whelps."

Zach, his face contorted by years of rage at such insults, tossed his pistol onto the ground and flew at Cal, his fists flying. "Aahyee!"

The surprise of his attack rewarded him with the first two blows, both flush hits, but after the second punch connected with Cal's nose, drawing his cork and spattering blood in every direction, the larger man delivered a jab that landed solidly in Zach's solar plexus.

Gasping for breath, Zach backed away momentarily, and when he did, Cal rushed toward the firearm on the ground.

"Touch it and you die!" Vincent warned, cocking his own pistol.

The bully stopped in his tracks.

"Move away," Vincent said, "this is one mill you will fight fairly."

Cal wiped the sleeve of his nightshirt across his face, momentarily stanching the blood that gushed from his nostrils; then he turned slowly and glared at Vincent, pure venom in his hooded eyes. "You want some of what I give him? Come and get it."

Vincent looked to Zach. "What say you? Shall I take him?"

Zach shook his head. "No! Keep your distance. He's mine."

Shrugging his broad shoulders, Vincent turned back to Aylesworth. "I shall wait my turn. For the moment, I bow to Mr. Flynn's prior claim."

Having regained his breath, Zach stepped forward again. With his fists held in front of him in an unschooled, yet effective manner, he skipped from foot to foot, moving about and ducking his head, making it difficult for Cal to get in a good punch at him. Vincent decided it was as Franny had said, Zach might choose not to fight, but he was not afraid to do so, not when the stakes were high enough.

Cal swung first, but Zach ducked, then he dealt the larger man a blow to the ribs that made him stagger back, his hamlike hand held to his side.

"That's for Franny," Zach said. "You've hit her for the last time. You touch her again, and I'll bury you."

"That so? Mayhap we'll see who buries who."

With his fists up, Zach skipped forward again, ready to fight. Unfortunately, Cal got in another flush hit to the solar plexus. This time, Zach was unable to catch his breath. He fell to his knees, and while he was down, Cal drew back his booted foot and kicked him in the groin.

Watching Zach Flynn as he fell over, moaning and writhing in pain, Vincent set his pistol lock at half-cock, then bent down and placed it on the ground. "My turn, I believe."

Cal whirled around, a grin upon his coarse face. "Come ahead, you fribble. Shall I queer your daylights, same as I did for that Bartholomew baby who was with my sister? Or," he said, pointing toward Zach and laughing, "do you fancy a dose of that medicine?"

"I shall choose neither of those unhappy alternatives. But you may try what you will. It is of little matter, for you will soon find that I am not so young as the lad, nor so trusting as Zach Flynn. I have met your like before. A man may travel to the remotest countries of the planet, and still he will meet just such a one as you—*un hombre malo*—a coward too stupid to occupy himself in any other way than by terrorizing those who are smaller and weaker."

"Coward, is it?"

"Yes. And an exceedingly stupid one at that."

Cal growled and muttered a vile name. "You've breathed your last," he said. Holding up his fists, he taunted Vincent to come closer.

Vincent inclined his head in a slight bow. "You first, Coward." Then, assuming a wide stance, with his knees slightly bent, he waited for the onslaught.

While Cal rushed forward like an enraged bull, Vincent stood his ground, unmoving until the last instant. Like a matador, he stepped aside unharmed, at the same time spinning around and hammering a two-handed blow between the big man's shoulders that knocked him to the ground, his face in the dirt.

Never doubting the efficacy of his maneuver, Vincent strolled over to where the giant lay, moaning but otherwise still. After putting his foot on that hamlike hand, on the chance that Cal might move, Vincent bent down and pressed his forefinger into the side of the fallen man's neck, continuing the pressure for about ten seconds. At the end of that time, he stepped away, leaving the village coward sprawled, unconscious upon the ground.

Zach, his breathing still ragged, picked himself up and staggered over to stand beside Cal's motionless body. After prodding the man with his foot to make certain he was, indeed, down for the count, he turned to Vincent. "How . . . how did you do that?"

"I employed a little trick I learned some years ago. I try not to use it too often, but when I do, I find it a most effective tool in lightening heavy work."

"Most effective," Zach agreed, looking at the still prostrate man. Returning his attention to the face that was so much like his own, he asked hesitantly, "would you teach it to me? If I am destined for prison, I suspect I'll have need of such a tool."

With Zach's help, Vincent managed to bundle Cal into the Stanhope and cart him over the bridge to the two large oak trees on the bank of the brook. After using his knife to borrow a length of the rope that was still tied between the oaks, he and Zach lashed Cal to the larger of the trees, the man's arms hugging the prickly circumference and his hairy stomach flush against the bark.

"You appear to be dancing with the tree," Zach said, not hiding his pleasure at Cal's predicament.

"Uermmh, uermmh," the man mumbled angrily, the handkerchief tied around his mouth making all but the most rudimentary sounds impossible.

Laughing, Zach picked up the nightshirt that lay on the ground. "I regret that I will not be here on the morrow when the first fair-goers discover you all trussed up like a Christmas goose, and naked as the day you were born."

"Uermmh!"

"You know we cannot stay," Vincent said, "for we must be on the road to London as soon as possible."

Taking the bloody nightshirt from Zach, he tossed it into the brook. "The distance to Town is a good forty miles, and covering it will require the better part of the morning. That leaves us scarcely twenty-four hours to contact the proper authorities and get this whole sordid business straightened out. Otherwise, I shall be obliged to meet young Neville's grandfather at dawn on Saturday at Hampstead Heath, where he will be waiting, ready and willing to avenge his grandson by putting a bullet through me."

"I haven't forgotten," Zach answered quietly. "I gave you my word, and I will not go back on it. I was merely enjoying the thought of Cal's coming humiliation. Though I doubt the experience will have any good effect upon his manners, the sight of his naked backside lashed to a tree should gratify any number of people who've known the brunt of his bullying."

"I daresay you are right. Let them draw such enjoyment from that as they may. In the meantime, let us fetch Franny and be on our way."

Chapter 14

Vincent tossed the quill onto his desk, then wadded the notepaper into a tight ball and threw it in the general direction of the fireplace. Landing short, the missile rolled beneath a maroon leather-covered wing chair. Deuce take it! this letter was proving almost as difficult to compose as the speech he had delivered before the Royal Academy yesterday afternoon. Of course, speaking to several hundred gentlemen and scholars had been nothing compared to writing to one brown-eyed female.

The gentlemen of the Academy had listened politely to Vincent's introductory speech; then, as he began to read from Lord Chester's research papers, they had become enthralled. The applause at the end of the two hours had been thunderous, and at least three publishers had asked if they might call upon him to discuss the publication of the papers and Lord Chester's exemplary drawings.

"Unfortunately," he said, pushing back his chair and stepping over to the ground-floor window that overlooked Brook Street, "I am not such a fool as to believe the lady will greet my words with similar indulgence."

While Vincent observed a hackney carriage pull up outside his town house, and dispatch its one passenger, he heard a soft knock at the library door.

"Enter," he called.

After a liveried footman opened the door, Franny Aylesworth fairly floated across the maroon and blue Axminster carpet. She looked even more beautiful than Vincent could have imagined, dressed in an emerald green traveling dress adorned with blond lace down the long sleeves and around the flounce of the skirt. Upon her golden curls sat a frothy confection of tulle and lace that exactly matched her green eyes.

Vincent crossed the room to meet her. "My dear, you are *très ravissante.*"

Franny curtsied, then held her hand out for Vincent to view the small, yet tasteful, emerald and diamond engagement ring upon her finger. "Is it not perfect?" she asked. "I never thought to own such jewelry."

"You are worth every stone, my dear, and more."

A blush stained her pretty cheeks. "Your lordship is too good. In fact, you are the most wonderful gentleman in all of England."

Brushing aside her praise, he stepped over to the pale marble mantelpiece, where a nosegay of roses, handsomely positioned within a silver filigree holder, lay beside the ormolu clock. "You have a wedding gift. It only just arrived."

"A gift? For me?"

He presented her with the flowers. "From your latest admirer, who wishes you all happiness in your new life."

Her eyes moist with tears, Franny took the flowers, sniffed the heady bouquet, then crushed the nosegay to her heart.

"They are from young Mr. Neville," Vincent said, handing her the card.

Franny looked at the white pasteboard, then asked Vincent if he would be so kind as to read her what was written.

"The young gentleman writes that the roses will pale beside your fair beauty, and that when he awoke to see you standing beside his sick bed, he thought he had slipped from this mortal coil and gone directly to heaven."

"La, my lord, did you ever in your life hear such pretty words?"

With a teasing smile, Vincent asked, "Are you quite certain, my dear, that you still wish to align yourself with that scoundrel, Zach Flynn? I suspect you need only smile at Mr. Neville to have him at your feet."

"I know you are teasing me, sir, so I'll not answer your question. I'll say only how glad I am that the young gentleman was able to set the story straight about it being a gang of street ruffians who dragged him into the alley and beat him senseless."

"Yes," Vincent replied, "once he saw Zach and Sir Burton standing together, it came back to him how it was those two who had rescued him and put him into the hackney."

A second knock sounded at the library door, and the old butler shuffled into the room, in his hand a silver tray bearing a visiting card. "The Reverend Glissome, my lord."

Not bothering with the card, Vincent bade the butler show the gentleman in.

Turning to Franny, he said, "I trust you are ready to become Mrs. Flynn."

Franny hugged the flowers to her pretty bosom, her green eyes as bright as the gems upon her hand. "Oh, your lordship, can this be real? All last night, while I lay abed, I kept pinching myself, afeared I'd wake to find I'd dreamed the whole. My new clothes, the wedding, the private cabin aboard the ship, it's all more than a body can take in."

Vincent squeezed her hand, then went to greet the Reverend Mr. Glissome. "Sir," he said, shaking the gentleman's hand, "how kind of you to come."

"Happy to be of service, Lord Thornton. And if I may say so, 'tis a beautiful day for a wedding. A good omen, don't you know."

The amenities completed, Vincent patted his coat to make certain he was still in possession of the special license and the wedding ring. He was. They reposed in his pocket next to the letter to his Aunt Letitia—a missive he had spent the better part of last evening composing.

He smiled, wishing he could see the expression on his aunt's face when the lady discovered that at the ripe old age of thirty-nine, and with a husband and a growing family filling the house to overflowing, she was suddenly in need of a paid companion.

For now, however, Vincent had other duties to perform. He must first find the prospective groom, then see the couple safely married and aboard the afternoon packet bound for America. When those tasks were completed, he could return to the town house and tackle once again the letter to a certain brown-eyed young lady.

Janine gazed out the near-side window of the chaise as they passed by the remains of yet another ancient Roman city. This one was a particularly interesting specimen, however, for upon a hillside she spied parts of a Roman theater, including a colonnaded stage, while in the distance, a fine stretch of city wall bisected the green, undulating landscape.

Not that she was as charmed by the sights as she had been three days ago when she had hugged Miss Evangeline and Miss Edwina farewell and left Bexham. The journey had been long, and even in the well-sprung traveling coach Gareth's mother had been so obliging as to send to convey her newly hired companion to Herefordshire—a gesture as kind as it was unexpected—the excitement of viewing new scenery and uncommonly beautiful countryside had begun to pall. Even knowing they were completing the last leg of the trip did not imbue it with any extraordinary charm.

She and her traveling companion—another unheard-of show of thoughtfulness on her new employer's part—had stopped for a light nuncheon and a change of horses at The Fighting Cocks Inn, on the outskirts of the cathedral town of Hereford, and as the postilion had put up the steps, he promised they would be in Shurdbury before three of the clock. "It be but a mere fifteen miles more to the Hall," he had said.

"I wish I knew the time," Janine said, more to herself than to Gareth's old nanny, the gray-haired woman who sat opposite her, those ever-present knitting needles *clickity-clickity-clicking* in rhythm to the rattle of the carriage wheels. More than once in the last three days, Janine had been forced to quell an almost overpowering temptation to wrest from the woman those clicking implements, as well as the ever-growing afghan, and fling the lot out the window.

"It be after two, Miss," replied the nanny in that same placid, almost bovine, manner she had sustained for the entire journey.

Janine blinked. Had the woman been in possession of a timepiece all along, and kept the information to herself?

Using a recently freed knitting needle, she pointed out the far-side window to a meadow filled with scarlet pimpernel. "See them pimpernel, Miss? The flowers be closed."

After waiting for a full minute, Janine said, "And that signifies?"

"They close up if rain be coming, or if it be two of the clock. 'Course, they'll close up if a body picks 'em too. But only a fool would bother picking pimpernel."

With nothing to add to this bit of country lore, Janine gave her attention to the early June landscape once again; it had changed steadily as the coach had progressed from Bexham to London, then from London to Bath. Turning northward, they had passed a number of lovely orchards in full flower and several interesting stretches of coppiced woodlands—the shoots of the birch, oak, and hornbeam all in bright green leaf. And once they had crossed the fast-moving River Wye, there had been the Roman ruins and pleasant little villages with their charming mud-and-timber cottages. At last, they had come to Hereford, with Shurdbury the next, and final, stop.

Janine might have enjoyed the entire trip if she had not been consumed with anxiety regarding this new position as Mrs. Henley's companion. As if from out of the blue, the letter from Gareth's mother had arrived, asking Janine if she was still free to entertain offers of employment.

Still free? Janine was not only free, she had been beside herself wondering what she would do if she did not soon hear from one of the agencies she had queried. And though she had been jubilant at the unexpected proposition, still, something about it niggled at her brain. Mrs. Henley was a relatively young woman, with a husband, a son, and a daughter to keep her busy. What need had she for a companion?

After the gentlemen had left Morgan House—an event that occurred in the small hours of the morning, while Janine slept—she and Miss Evangeline and Chloe had returned to Bexham, to Dyrham cottage. There they had stayed.

Even after Miss Edwina's wedding had come and gone, and the newly married lady had moved to St. Anne's rectory with her *worthy* new husband, Janine had remained at the cottage. Though she had written letters of inquiry to employment agencies in London and Bath, she had received no replies, and every day she had grown more desperate to find a means of supporting herself. But what was worse—what still ate away at her heart, like acid dripping upon a stone—was that she had not heard a word from any of the four men who had stolen away in the dark of the night.

No, not *men*. One man.

She cared not a farthing what had become of Sir Burton and Zach Flynn, and as for Mr. Gareth Henley, that injured gentleman's fate was of only humanitarian interest to her. It was Vincent whose disappearance tore at her insides . . .Vincent whose continued absence drained the very life force from her soul.

Never mind that he had returned to Morgan House to fetch his cousin and her brother, and that he had told Miss Evangeline where they were bound. He had not said good-bye to Janine, and it was that fact which cut up her peace.

That, and the fear that she would never see him again as long as she lived!

"The Hall be just around the next bend."

"What?" Lost in her own misery, Janine had not been attending the words of her traveling companion.

"It be round the next bend," Nanny Whitfield repeated. "Henley Hall. The finest house in all Herefordshire."

There was a perceptible slackening of the horses' pace, and as they rounded the next bend, Janine saw a low stone wall and a handsome, well-cared for gatehouse. Perched on the wall was a freckle-faced lad of about ten or eleven, who appeared to have been awaiting their arrival, for at sight of the coach, the grinning boy waved his hand, then ran to fling open the wrought-iron gates.

As the coach drew past the gatehouse and continued down the curving gravel carriageway, Janine was treated to a perfect view of the house. The nanny may have exaggerated when she declared Henley Hall the finest house in Herefordshire, but it was a lovely edifice by anyone's standards.

Grand and dignified, yet somehow welcoming, it's four stories and two wings were timbered and constructed of mellowed pink stone, with diamond-pane windows arranged in pairs all along the front of the building. To add a further bit of stateliness, a motto was carved above the columns which supported the upper part of the building, and as the horses drew to a standstill before the portico, Janine was able to see the writing clearly.

I shall prevail, it read.

"And so shall I," she muttered. No matter that her heart was heavy and her spirits low, she would somehow overcome those feelings. She must!

A new position as companion, no matter how convivial it might turn out to be, was not what Janine had envisioned for her future. In the few days she and Vincent had spent together at Morgan House, she had come to hope—nay, believe—that the two of them would unite in love and travel life's road together, their hearts fulfilling one another's dreams, as their bodies fulfilled one another's . . .

She was forced to thrust such thoughts from her mind, for the front door was thrown open and a beautiful blond woman in her late thirties stepped outside, a smile of welcome upon her face. Her resemblance to her son, Gareth, was unmistakable, for here, in the feminine form, were the same clear blue eyes, the same angelic fairness, the same happy disposition as Gareth possessed.

"My dear," Letitia Henley said above the noise of the coachman's orders to the postilion to quit his gawking and jump down from the roof of the coach to assist the passengers. "How pleased I am that you are here at last."

The lady waited only until the chastised postilion let down the steps and helped Janine to alight, then she came forward, her hands outstretched as if welcoming an old friend.

Not knowing what else to do, Janine placed her hands in those of her new employer. To her further surprise, she felt herself being pulled close and soundly embraced.

Once she was free, she curtsied. "How do you do, Mrs. Henley? I must thank you for your solicitousness in sending not only the coach and the outriders, but Nanny Whitfield as well."

"You are more than welcome, I am sure, my dear. But let us have no more of this *Mrs. Henley* business, for I refuse to stand upon ceremony with you. I mean for us to be fast friends, so you must begin by calling me Letitia."

Janine could not think how to reply to such condescension. She had called Cousin Hortense by her name, of course, but that was understandable. Although they were employer and employee, they were also first cousins once removed. However, Letitia Henley was a complete stranger to her. How could she presume to address the lady with such informality? It smacked of a familiarity—a relationship—that did not exist.

"Ma'am, I—"

"By Jove!" called a young gentleman who had just come galloping up the carriageway on a handsome gray mare. "Miss Morgan. Well met!"

Gareth Henley jumped down and came to her, his hand outstretched, and while Janine listened to his words of welcome, she allowed herself a quick look to see how his handsome face had fared after the beating he had suffered four weeks ago. Happily, it retained only the slightest reminders of that brutalization, a slight discoloration beneath the eye and a small, angry cut across the bottom lip.

"I collect," he said, noticing her inspection, "that you are curious as to my recovery."

"Forgive my rudeness, sir, but I wished to satisfy myself that you had sustained no permanent injury. I hope I see you in much better health than when we last met."

"You do, ma'am. The apothecary removed Chloe's neat stitches only this morning, and I am happy to inform you that my ribs are healing nicely." He displayed the boyish, cheeky grin that had been so much in evidence when he was at Morgan House. "So nicely, in fact, that I am no longer required to hug myself before I sneeze."

Laughing, Janine said, "Miss Evangeline will be quite pleased to hear of your progress."

"Ah, the inestimable Miss Craven. When you write

to that lady," he said, "pray tell her for me, *Vis medica-trix naturae.*"

"Bah," declared his mother, "such talk." Then turning to Janine, she said, "You need write no such thing, my dear! I warn you, you must pay no attention to my son's whimsies. His father and I must put up with them, of course, for he is our only son, but you need feel no such constraints."

Gareth rolled his eyes heavenward, as if much put upon, and Janine smiled at the friendly by-play between mother and son. How pleasant to be in the bosom of a family once again.

"Thank you, ma'am, for giving me leave to decline the office. Firstly, Mr. Henley's message sounds suspiciously like Latin, and I should never be able to spell the words. Secondly, I distinctly remember hearing him accuse Miss Evangeline of exposing him to a fever of the brain by quoting to him from that language. And thirdly, since I also remember how often she called him a disrespectful pup, I am not at all certain that he has not bid me say something thoroughly disgraceful to my best friend."

The gentleman was about to defend himself against such maligning when his mother proposed that he do his own dirty work. "For Janine wants no part of your silly dead language."

"But I could spell it out for her, and—"

"Desist!" said his beleaguered parent.

Linking her arm through Janine's, the lady led her toward the entrance. "How typical of the male sex," she said. "Just let a man decide to pepper his conversation with Latin, and he naturally assumes that the rest of us will be enraptured to follow suit." She leaned close to Janine and lowered her voice. "I do not mind, actually, for he has adopted the habit only because my nephew is forever muttering something in Spanish. You must know, Vincent is Gareth's hero."

At the mention of Vincent's name, Janine was overcome with such loneliness that she felt as if an unseen hand had reached inside her chest and yanked out her heart, leaving a gaping hole where that life-sustaining organ used to be.

"Did someone call my name?"

"Vincent, dear boy," said his aunt, looking to the right of the portico. "As usual, your timing is impeccable."

Chapter 15

Letitia Henley unlinked her arm from Janine's and beckoned for Vincent to come and take her place. "I wondered where you could be," she said.

"I was enjoying a turn in your rose garden," he replied, and though his words were for his aunt, his gaze was fastened upon the face of the new arrival.

Not at all offended by such rude behavior, his aunt said, "I am glad you have come, dear boy, for I wish you will escort Janine inside for me while I speak with Nanny Whitfield."

"My pleasure, ma'am."

Janine watched Vincent bound up the half dozen steps, moving in that powerful, yet graceful way that was so much a part of him, and try as she might, she could not avert her gaze. She had never seen him look more handsome. He was clad in a beautifully tailored coat of Devonshire brown, with buff pantaloons that hugged his powerful thighs, and a cream and blue striped waistcoat that lent a touch of the summer sky to his gray eyes, and dressed thus, he appeared exactly what he was, a gentleman of wealth and taste.

Though she should have expected it, Janine was unprepared for his clean-shaven face, for with his strong chin and his angular jaw line exposed to view, he was at once the man she knew and a complete stranger.

Without saying a word, he made her a bow, then caught her hand and placed it on his arm, much as he had done the day of the fair. The instant she touched him, Janine discovered the error of that earlier sensation regarding an unseen hand reaching inside her chest and yanking out her heart. That life-sustaining organ still resided in its rightful place, for it had begun to pound with such force she wondered why no one remarked upon the noise.

Wanting to cover the sound of the heartbeats, yet feeling decidedly ill-at-ease with this familiar stranger, she said the first thing that entered her head. "You are well, sir?"

"I am. And you, ma'am?"

"I am well also."

They had entered the hall—a spacious rotunda with a beige and green Italian marble floor and a delicately wrought circular staircase that seemed to hang suspended upon nothing but the air—when Vincent broke the next stretch of silence. "And Miss Craven?" he asked. "I hope you left that lady in good spirits."

"Yes, thank you. Quite good."

"Good. And Jezebel? How does she fare?"

"I am pleased to relate that the creature is still within her allotted nine lives."

Thankfully, before they were reduced to discussing the equine population, the elder Mr. Henley put in an appearance, descending that fragile-looking staircase with a speed and daring that made Janine hold her breath, lest he miss his footing and pitch headlong to the floor below.

"Ah," he said, a smile of greeting upon his pleasant, though unremarkable face. "Miss Morgan, I presume."

Safely arrived at the bottom stair, the middle-aged gentleman saluted her hand, then begged to be allowed to show her into the morning room. "Our good Mrs.

Quincey has only just sent in tea, and since I am all too well acquainted with the quality of the food to be had at posting inns, I am persuaded you must be starved."

Though Janine could have told him how much more palatable were the meals served at posting inns than those put before passengers traveling upon the stage, she refrained. "Actually, sir, I partook of a delicious nuncheon but a few hours ago."

"Even so, my dear, I insist you join us, for we shall all have need of sustenance. I must inform you that we have deemed it expedient to forgo our regular family dinner, so the servants may use their time to assist in the preparation for the ball."

"The ball?" Janine only just managed to squeak out the words.

"I beg your pardon, my dear. I did not mean to startle you with my little joke. Actually, one could be forgiven for thinking it a ball, so busy as the servants have been these past few days, but 'tis only a party in honor of my wife's fortieth birthday. There will be dancing, of course, but nothing on a grand scale. Did no one tell you?"

"No, sir. I had no idea. How ill-timed of me to arrive on such a day."

"Nonsense, my dear. We have invited upwards of sixty people, so of what consequence is one more guest? Especially," he added, patting her hand in an avuncular manner, "when it is one whose arrival has been so anxiously awaited."

Not knowing how to respond to a remark which she felt certain had been spoken for the sole purpose of putting her at her ease, Janine kept her thoughts to herself, allowing the gentleman to show her into the cozy gold and yellow morning room, where he bid her make herself comfortable in a bronze brocade wing chair. He was drawing up one of a set of fruitwood nested tables for her use when Vincent and the rest of the party entered the room.

The Henleys—mother, son, and fourteen-year-old Maryanne, all divinely fair—were a thoroughly loquacious lot. And while Janine sat quietly, observing the cheerful interchange between the family members—all save Lord Thornton, who uttered scarcely a word, yet stared at her in a manner she was at a loss to understand—she pretended to partake of the sumptuous tea. After nibbling at only one of the dozens of assorted sandwiches, she chose a single sweet from the platter of fruit tarts and sugar cakes, refusing altogether a dish of strawberries fresh from Mr. Henley's forcing house.

In reality, Janine feared she might choke upon the food, for she still reeled from the sudden and totally unexpected appearance of her new employer's nephew. As well, she was much too aware of Lord Thornton's presence in the room to do more than listen, eyes downcast, to the list of delights in store for the party-goers that evening.

When at last the meal was finished, Janine ventured to suggest that she remain in her room until morning, using fatigue from the journey as her excuse for not joining the birthday celebration. Unfortunately, neither Mr. nor Mrs. Henley would hear of such a thing.

"Nonsense," Letitia Henley informed her. "You must not miss the party."

"But, ma'am, I—"

"Please," the lady said, reaching forward and seizing Janine's hand, "you cannot mean to disappoint me on my birthday. Besides," she added, as though Janine's acquiescence was a foregone conclusion, "all has been taken care of, so you need only rest upon your bed for an hour or two, to recoup your strength, then join us at quarter to eight for a private toast before the guests arrive."

"You shall enjoy the evening prodigiously," Mr. Henley assured her.

In no position to refuse the invitation, Janine gave in as gracefully as possible. "I shall look forward to it, sir."

The words had no sooner left Janine's lips than her employer bade the butler, who stood near the door should he be needed, show Miss Morgan to her room. Within minutes she was whisked up those mystically suspended stairs to a beautifully appointed front bedchamber decorated in shades of celestial blue and muted silver, where Bess, an apple-cheeked young housemaid, waited to assist her.

"Afternoon, Miss. I only just this minute finished filling the hip bath. So if it please you, I'll help you out of your traveling clothes straight away."

Janine gazed longingly at the steaming water, while the maid stepped forward and began to divest her of her pelisse and frock. Within minutes she was lolling in the bath, the water lapping gently against her skin, relieving her taut muscles.

And taut they were, though the circumstance resulted not from the day's travel, but from the hour spent sitting in the morning room with Vincent staring at her. She had been seated only inches away from him, yet prohibited from broaching any subject of a personal nature, and that alone was enough to cause her muscles to rebel.

Not that Vincent had appeared particularly desirous of introducing a personal subject. On the contrary, he seemed quite content to let his relatives dictate the course of the conversation.

Janine sighed. All this time she had been waiting, hoping to hear some word from him, and when she finally found herself so close she could have reached out and touched him, Vincent appeared to have nothing whatever to say to her.

"Some oil of jasmine, Miss?"

Nodding her permission, Janine watched as the servant added several drops of the aromatic oil to the water. Never in her life had she known such pampering. Not even when her parents were alive had she enjoyed the services of a personal maid. And the room to which she had been shown was so far superior to the room she had called her own at her cousin Hortense's house in Bath, that to compare the two was to liken gold to coarse metal.

Totally mystified by such treatment, Janine expected at any moment to hear a knock at the chamber door, followed by the appearance of a butler, ready to move her to a smaller, less elegant room, explaining as he did so that a mistake had been made.

Of course, a mistake *had* been made, and Janine was very much afraid that it was she who had made it. She should not have come to Herefordshire—should not have come to the home of Vincent's aunt and uncle.

With Vincent choosing to treat her as a stranger—a circumstance that left her heartsore and feeling more alone than she had dreamed possible—how could she remain in a house where he was a frequent visitor? The answer to that question was simple. She could not.

It would seem that she had been in the right of it back in Bexham, when she told herself that a wealthy baron was above her touch. And yet, after seeing Vincent again, Janine realized she was as much in love with him as ever. And loving him as she did, she knew she could not meet him every day and pretend they were no more to one another than nodding acquaintances. She was not that strong; not that good at dissembling.

Realizing that the present situation was impossible,

Janine decided it was imperative that she find some excuse to decline Mrs. Henley's offer of employment. At the moment, however, she was too relaxed, too sleepy to think what that excuse might be.

"You'll be wanting a short nap," the maid said, holding Janine's wrapper so she could exchange it for the bath sheet.

"I want it," she agreed, "but I have not the time to spare. Mrs. Henley has insisted that I attend this evening's festivities, and I must see what can be done about a gown. Not that I have anything remotely suitable for a party where there is to be dancing."

"You don't need to worrit over that, Miss, for it's all been taken care of. The laundress is touching up your dress as we speak. You rest now, and I'll come and wake you when it's time to prepare for the party."

Thinking the servant had unpacked her pink sarcenet and taken it belowstairs to have it pressed, Janine gave in to her need for rest and climbed into the luxurious bed. In less time than it took to punch the eiderdown pillow into the appropriate shape, she was asleep.

When Bess returned two hours later, Janine awoke refreshed from her nap, but still none too comfortable about joining the family for the birthday fete. Actually, it might not have been quite so bad if Vincent were not one of the party, for when Janine had lived in Bath with her Cousin Hortense, she had learned how to hold her head up among strangers, even though she was not attired in the latest fashion. At the outset of her stay, she had learned not to put undue importance upon such matters.

However, tonight was different. She hated to appear shabby genteel before the man she loved, especially if it was to be the last time she ever saw him.

Knowing there was no way to escape the inevitable, Janine allowed Bess to help her into freshly pressed drawers and shift. Then, after donning her one pair of silk stockings, she sat submissively at a small, inlaid dressing table while the servant brushed her hair.

"It's lovely hair you've got, Miss, if you'll forgive my saying so. So long and shiny as it is, and the color of dark, sweet chocolate." Her commentary at an end, the maid caught the thick mass in both hands, twisting the whole several turns. When her task was completed, she employed a pair of tortoise-shell combs to secured the simple coiffure high upon Janine's head.

"Oh, my," Janine said, gazing at her reflection in the looking glass. "How . . . how pretty. You are very talented."

" 'Tis easy enough to hit upon a pleasing style," Bess said, arranging a few saucy little curls around Janine's face, "when a body's got tresses like yours."

Upon hearing a faint scratch at the chamber door, the artist gave her work a final pat. "That'll be your dress, Miss."

While stealing a second look at the elegantly arranged hair, Janine overheard the maid mutter something to an unseen person in the corridor. "I'll take it from here," she said. After dismissing the other servant, Bess returned, pushing the door shut with her hip.

Expecting to see the familiar pink sarcenet, Janine was startled to discover something entirely different draped across the woman's outstretched arms. It was a delectable confection of amber-shot tussore silk, whose square neckline and short sleeves were banded by double layers of filet lace dyed a chocolate brown.

"There's a wrap with it, Miss. Made of gauze as sheer as a spider's web, it is, but I can't think you'll be needing it on such a lovely night."

Janine stared at the gown, mesmerized by its simple beauty, wishing it did, indeed, belong to her, for it suited perfectly both her taste and coloring. "I fear there has been a mistake," she said, reaching out to touch the shimmering silk. "The gown is not mine."

Bess blinked as if unable to understand the words. "But of course it's yours, Miss. The bandbox come about a week ago, and the mistress had me bring it directly to your room." She held up a pair of satin slippers. "These came with it."

"You must have misunderstood. I am persuaded the dress belongs to Mrs. Henley. Something for her birthday, perhaps."

"With her fair looks? Not likely. Wearing pale blue, the mistress is, to go with the new sapphire necklace the master gave her. This here color is for a lady with dark hair, like yourself."

After an argument that lasted for several minutes, Janine decided she would be obliged to don the confection just to prove to the maid that it could not be hers. It was she who received the surprise, however, for when all the tiny silk-covered buttons were secured up the back, the gown fit as though it had been made for her.

"Now then, Miss. You see it's just as I told you. They was meant for you all along."

Before Janine could say more, Miss Maryanne Henley tapped at the door, then peeped around the corner to tell her the guests would be arriving any minute. "Oh, you look lovely," the young lady said. "But do hurry. Mother is a dear about most things, but she is an absolute Tartar about punctuality."

Unable to think what was best to do, Janine allowed herself to be pushed out into the corridor, though she followed at a much more decorous pace than Miss Maryanne, refusing to emulate that young lady's frighteningly fast descent down the circular staircase.

The hall had been transformed since early afternoon. Candles burned brightly in the crystal chandelier and in all the sconces, and along the curving walls of the rotunda the tapestry benches had been removed to accommodate dozens of tubs filled with flowering shrubs, the heady perfume of their blossoms floating upon the air. As well, a hauntingly sweet melody played by pianoforte, violin, and cello drifted from the rear of the house, from what Janine guessed must be the ballroom.

Since no one had told her where the family would meet, she followed the sound of the music. Drawing near its source, she spied Vincent and Gareth Henley standing in an archway, their backs to the hall.

The two gentlemen—one divinely fair, the other devilishly dark and handsome—were both attired in evening clothes, and while Janine paused a moment to enjoy the sight of Vincent, resplendent in darkest blue, she overheard them speaking of someone.

"I meant no offense," Gareth hurried to assure his cousin. "When I said she would make you a *handsome* baroness, I thought it was an acceptable epithet for a lady no longer in her first blush of youth."

Baroness! Vincent had chosen a wife!

Janine felt as if someone had just driven a knife through her heart.

"You betray your immaturity," Vincent said somewhat sharply. "Believe me, the lady's beauty has only just begun to bloom."

"Of . . . of course, Cousin."

"Some women," Vincent continued more calmly, "are like a work of art—a painting created by the hand of a master. As you know, any dilettante can splash color upon a canvas, but when a true master takes up palette and brush, he puts something between the canvas and the paint—he bestows upon his creation heart, depth, soul. Such a work lives forever, its beauty undimmed.

"So it is with a few very special women. They possess depth and character, and though the years pass, their beauty never fades."

Hearing Vincent's words, the passion in his voice, Janine felt her body begin to tremble. It was difficult to draw breath, and she was forced to bite her lip to keep the tears at bay.

To speak thus of a woman, he must love her with all his heart, and with all his soul.

At the thought of him loving another with such intensity, a pain rent Janine to the very core of her being. Fearing she might faint, she looked around her, seeking a place to sit before she humiliated herself by collapsing on the floor. Unfortunately, every chair had been removed to accommodate the flowering shrubs, and she was reduced to leaning against the wall.

She had only just reached out for the support when she heard Vincent's voice.

"*Querida!*" he said, rushing to her side. "What is wrong, *mi amor?*"

"Vincent, I . . ."

The room seemed to tilt, and Janine braced herself, expecting to feel the hard marble floor come up to meet her. To her immense relief, the object with which she collided was not the floor, but a man's rock-hard chest, and as she collapsed against Vincent, she felt his strong arms wrap around her, pulling her close. In an instant he had scooped her up as if she weighed no more than a stone, and carried her off to some place in the far recesses of the house, a place where the sweet scent of flowers no longer teased her nostrils and the music no longer filled her ears.

Not that she cared where he took her.

It was enough, for the moment, to be in his arms again, held fast against his chest. More than enough to be able to wind her arms around his neck and lay her head upon his broad shoulder. She felt his heart beating, its accelerated rhythm matching her own so perfectly that for an instant she wondered if her heart had stopped altogether.

Vincent entered a small, book-strewn room, lit by a single brace of candles, then still holding her, he seated himself in the only chair the room boasted. Thankfully, it was a large chair, capable of accommodating two people, for he made himself comfortable, and without asking her opinion upon the subject, pulled his arms even tighter around her, molding her body to fit his.

Since Janine had no objection to such high-handed treatment, she snuggled contentedly against him, settling her face into the hollow of his shoulder and breathing deeply of the clean, fresh smell of him.

They sat thus for several minutes, then finally Vincent asked gently, "All better, my love?"

My love. Janine thrilled to the whispered endearment, but in the next instant she remembered that she had no right to his soft words. He had chosen another as his future bride. Hardening her heart, she said, "I told you not to call me that."

"True, *querida*, and as much as I wish to please you in all things, something inside me will not let me obey that particular stricture."

Janine could not believe her ears. "You want to please me?"

"But, of course, my love."

She pushed away from him only far enough to allow herself to look into his face. "But what of your intended bride—the *handsome* lady you and Gareth were discussing when I . . . I . . . ?"

"When you eavesdropped?" he asked, resignation in his voice.

Janine had the grace to blush. "I could not help but overhear."

"If you must listen in upon other people's conversations, my sweet, I wish you would arrive in time to hear the whole. The lady of whom we were speaking was none other than yourself."

Not certain she had heard him correctly, she said, "The lady you likened to a painting by a master? That was me?"

"Of course. Who did you suppose it to be?"

"I thought surely you referred to some lady of the *ton*. Someone worthy of becoming your baroness."

"Worthy? What foolishness is this?"

When she did not answer, he sighed. "In my life, I have had two saviors. The first was Lord Chester, who saved me from the cane fields and from the anger that was devouring me from within."

"And the second?" she asked quietly.

"The second was a lady who stumbled into my life during a rainstorm. Though she came in looking like a drowned rat, soaked through to the skin, her spirit was filled with sunshine, and just being with her lightened the darkness that permeated my soul. She was trusting, and brave, and loyal, and loving, and even without money or a home, she was filled with hope for a better future. Soon, without my knowing how or when, she stole her way into my heart, imbuing it with all those qualities she had in abundance. And in so doing, she saved me from a life without love. Would you not call such a one worthy?"

Receiving no answer to his question, he lifted her hand and placed a soft, warm kiss inside her palm. "*Te quiero*," he whispered.

Too overwhelmed by what he had said about her, and unable to stem the flood of warmth that spread through her body at his kiss, Janine concentrated upon his last remark. "In my next life," she said, "I shall have the foresight to learn Spanish."

His lips moved from her palm to the inside of her wrist, lingering upon the wildly beating pulse. "I said only that I love you."

"But you cannot love me. You are a baron, and I am only a—"

Vincent put an end to her protest by covering her mouth with his own. He kissed her gently at first, lest he frighten her, but when she wound her arms around his neck and pressed her soft breast against his chest, responding to him with an abandon that caused his blood to catch fire, he crushed her in his arms and kissed her as he had longed to do from almost the first minute he met her.

He kissed her passionately, ardently, trailing kisses across her satiny face, then upon her dewy eyelids, before returning once again to her delectable mouth. After a time, however, when he deemed it prudent to bring this captivating pastime to an end, he gently disentangled himself from her embrace, clasping her by the shoulders and holding her at arm's length.

"My love," he whispered, "there is something I need to ask you."

She sighed contentedly, then opened her beautiful brown eyes, looking at him with such love in her expression that he was hard-pressed not to kiss her again.

"You may ask me anything," she said, "but I think I should much rather be kissed again."

"You shall be kissed as much as you like, once you have agreed to become my wife."

"Your wife?"

"Yes. And the sooner the better, for I love you, and I want to spend the rest of my life with you. That is, if you love me too."

"I do love you," she said. "With all my heart."

Vincent could not remember ever being as happy as he was at that moment. The last shreds of his bitterness seemed to melt away, and he felt whole, complete. Hearing Janine's words of love, it was as though he had come home at last.

"And you will marry me?"

"Yes," she said, her eyes shining with joy. "I should like that very much."

When she turned her face up to seal the bargain with another kiss, he resisted the temptation, but only just, reminding her that the house would soon be filling with people. "I am afraid we must return to the party, my love, else people will remark our absence."

Janine did not try to hide her disappointment. "But you promised me another kiss. In my next life," she teased, "I shall . . ." She paused, for she had chanced to gaze into his gray eyes, beholding such love in their depths that it had put all other thoughts from her mind—all save the vision of the life they would soon share. A life filled with love.

"In your next life," he prompted.

She shook her head. "From this day on, I shall do as the fortune-teller suggested, and forget about my next life." Catching his face between her hands, she placed a kiss upon his lips. "From this moment," she said, "I shall concentrate upon my joyous present, and upon our wonderful future."

"Our future," he repeated softly, wondrously.

"A future," she added, settling herself once again against his chest, "spent with the man I love with all my heart."